## "How much do you know about alligators?"

Christian McCoid's question brought Jocasta abruptly out of her daydream.

Puzzled, Jocasta looked at her boss. Was this some kind of trick question? Or the start of a joke? Could he be about to embark on an anecdote before they settled down to business?

"Nothing," she replied. "Why?"

"Because there's a farmer who has one that he reckons is lovesick. Apparently the family keep it as a pet."

"You want me to do a story on that?" Jocasta asked, her enthusiasm cracking down to ground level with a deadening bump.

Christian nodded. "For St. Valentine's Day. We usually sign off on an amusing note and Al the alligator languishing for lack of love sounds perfect."

**ELIZABETH OLDFIELD** began writing professionally as a teenager after taking a mail-order writing course, of all things. She later married a mining engineer, gave birth to a daughter and a son and happily put her writing career on hold. Her husband's work took them to Singapore for five years, where Elizabeth found romance novels and became hooked on the genre. Now she's a full-time writer in Scotland and has the best of both worlds—a rich family life and a career that fits the needs of her husband and children.

## Books by Elizabeth Oldfield

HARLEQUIN PRESENTS
1212—SPARRING PARTNERS
1300—RENDEZVOUS IN RIO
1333—THE PRICE OF PASSION
1365—LOVE GAMBLE
1395—FLAWED HERO
1429—AN ACCIDENTAL AFFAIR

# ELIZABETH OLDFIELD

## stay until dawn

*Harlequin Books*

TORONTO • NEW YORK • LONDON
AMSTERDAM • PARIS • SYDNEY • HAMBURG
STOCKHOLM • ATHENS • TOKYO • MILAN
MADRID • WARSAW • BUDAPEST • AUCKLAND

Harlequin Presents first edition August 1992
ISBN 0-373-11484-2

Original hardcover edition published in 1991
by Mills & Boon Limited

STAY UNTIL DAWN

# CHAPTER ONE

THERE were good days when everything went swimmingly and without a hitch, and, thank goodness, they were in the majority. However, from time to time a rogue bad day sneaked in—like today.

Not long after the early morning car delivered Jocasta to the television studios it became apparent that the fates were conspiring against the smooth running of the breakfast programme, including her role in it. First the make-up girl dropped a blob of foundation down her shoulder, so the navy pea jacket she was wearing with matching trousers and sand-coloured shirt had had to be abandoned. Next came a warning that the first person she was due to interview had, so far, failed to arrive. Later, contact with the outside broadcast link was inexplicably lost. And, at the last minute when she had taken her place on the couch, the running order, which had already been chopped and changed, was hastily switched around again.

As the *First Watch* logo appeared on the monitor and the jaunty signature tune began to twing-twang out, Jocasta found herself wondering why someone who was, by nature, a night owl had ever agreed to work as a presenter on a seven-to-ten morning show. It was one of life's ironies. For her, talk in the early fragile hours ranked as a crime against humanity and had always jarred, so being brightly interested on screen demanded the utmost in discipline and will-power. And after a night when sleep had proved elusive and long hours had been spent conducting endless imagined conversations with an adversary—her eyes flickered up to the windows of the control room—it promised to be hell.

'Three, two, one—you have lift off,' a disembodied voice chanted through her earpiece, and Jocasta took a deep breath and superglued on a smile.

'Chaos!' Christian McCoid denounced three hours later, as the *First Watch* team assembled in his office for coffee, *beignets* and the usual post-mortem. Sweeping strands of floppy brown hair back from his brow, the news director glowered around the table. 'I accept some of it was my fault in that I've not been around as much as I should have lately, but another shoot like that and before you know it the plug'll be pulled on the damn programme.'

'*First Watch* could—could be axed?' Jocasta enquired, in startled alarm.

Stormy grey eyes swung to hers. 'To be replaced by repeats of *I Love Lucy,*' Christian said bitingly.

Her heart cramped. Although her preference might be to appear before the cameras at a later, more agreeable hour, the last thing she wanted was for the programme to end. No, thanks. No way. Not when it was only a month since she had quit her job with a regional TV company back in England and flown across the Atlantic to join the staff of TKFM, New Orleans' premier public communications station. Having been offered an opportunity to widen her experience, Jocasta had envisaged spending a year learning as much as she could and acquiring an international gloss, then returning as the highly sought-after prodigal daughter who would have the major British channels fighting for her services. But if her present appointment was terminated in double-quick time she would be in a very different position. Television was an intensely cut-throat competitive field, and to be associated with failure, no matter how fleetingly or if it was at a distance, raised question marks. Involuntarily she winced. Instead of her career advancing, it might well stall!

Beside her, Gaelene, the ever-cheerful black girl who had shared the couch that morning, noticed her distress.

'Don't worry,' she whispered, 'he's exaggerating. Occasionally, when he's under pressure, Mr Gorgeous erupts and goes a little wild. I figure the French blood which runs through his veins heats up, a head of steam gathers, then—wow!—it's volcano time.' She giggled. 'All that passion must make him a wonderful lover.'

'So the programme isn't in danger of folding?' Jocasta hissed.

'Never. The ratings are high, and now that you've replaced Debra they're destined to go even higher.'

'Thanks, I hope so.' She enjoyed a quiet moment of relief. 'Why is Christian under pressure?' she enquired, as the coffee and small, sugared, diamond-shaped doughnuts were circulated.

'Because after his organising a change of studios, I hear it's just been decided that the evening news show should have a new format; plus he's in the process of moving house himself. But also——' Gaelene flashed a regretful smile '—I reckon he's still uptight about the change in *First Watch*'s personnel.'

Jocasta sighed. From their first meeting the news director had been suspicious, disapproving and aloof. An initial antipathy was understandable—having an unseen and untried stranger dumped on him would have been aggravating to say the least—but surely by now he had realised she was a capable and committed television journalist? He must. Yet his attitude towards her had not eased. He might be on best-buddy terms with Gaelene and Barton Maynard, who made up the programme's trio of presenters—and with everyone else in the television and radio complex, come to that—but she was kept at barge-pole distance. He might dispatch her colleagues around Louisiana and to various of the other states where they reported on interesting topical events, but thus far Jocasta had been restricted to the studio and items such as leisure, fashion, food fads—which, in her opinion, resided on the small-fry, Mickey Mouse level. It was a level she had outgrown long ago.

Pensively, she sipped her coffee. In her night-time conversations with the phantom Christian McCoid, she had roundly rebuked him for his continuing wariness and insisted he was foolish

to waste the talents of a woman who possessed
magnificent potential—at which point he had
given an apologetic smile and humbly agreed.
Very humbly. Indeed, the tall American had
looked chastened, discomfited, broken.
Jocasta's blue eyes travelled along the table.
The man at its head was not broken now, she
thought wryly. On the contrary, he looked the
ultimate in powerful self-assurance. Sprawled
in a chair with one shirt-sleeved arm hooked
along its back, Christian was listening as Gavin,
his second in command and the person immediately responsible for the in-studio oper-
ation of *First Watch,* explained how a film
feature had, most confusingly, gone astray. His
pale grey eyes glittered with a critical light, his
face was stern, and as he listened the ballpoint
pen he held in his fingers beat out an impatient
tattoo on the teak table. Rap, rap, rap. Excuses, excuses, excuses, it said. These post-
programme retrospectives were normally re-
laxed, but Christian's displeasure had instilled
today's with all the tension of a visit to the
dentist.

Gaelene had christened him Mr Gorgeous,
Jocasta mused, as Gavin was severely casti-
gated and the next culprit selected. She took
another sip of coffee. Well...maybe. Although
he had a wide brow, straight nose and a firm

jaw, at first glance Christian McCoid was not matinée-idol handsome. However, his restless energy and a sense of in-built sophistication made certain you looked twice. Then the elegant slope of his shoulders was noticed, and his thick dark lashes, and the lips, which were as fine-chiselled as a Michelangelo statue. There were bronze lights in the burnished brown hair which curled on to his collar, and his skin possessed a pale cappuccino tint. Could that be due to his Gallic ancestry? she wondered. According to Gaelene, who crammed any spare minute with titbits of gossip, his father was New Orleans born and bred, while his mother came from Paris. Jocasta rested her chin on her hand. Christian's sophistication showed in his self-contained manner, in the way he dressed—his shirt was stark white and billowy, and although he wore the ubiquitous jeans they fitted immaculately—and in his work. All too often breakfast shows could be monotonous slabs of junk viewing interspersed with newscasts and time checks, and she had had her fears about *First Watch*. However, the programme came blessed with structure, varied content and style—thanks to Christian. Despite the evening news show's having the major call on his time, he made frequent and gimlet-eyed appearances to check on presentation and editing, and to issue the strong-minded manifestos which gave the programme his distinctive stamp.

'I said, what were you playing at?' a deep melodious voice repeated, and with a start Jocasta realised that the subject of her thoughts was now channelling his free-floating annoyance at her.

She flushed. 'Me?'

'If you remember,' Christian rasped, 'you introduced a clip which had already been vetoed and then, in a banal link, switched to Barton's outside broadcast a good ten seconds ahead of time.'

Jocasta's flush deepened. She did remember. For four weeks she had hardly put a foot wrong, but this morning she had been out of step. Disastrously. The only consolation was that everyone else had stumbled around, too. She frowned. She also remembered that, despite his antagonism, for four weeks Christian McCoid had been remorselessly polite and well-mannered; but now his tone was sarcastic. The gloves had come off, it seemed. Banal link? She considered that, in the circumstances, she had been surprisingly eloquent!

'The talkback facility had broken,' Jocasta started, in self-defence.

'I'm aware of that,' he grated.

'And when someone waved a piece of paper at me I read the wrong number, and so read the wrong script.'

'Easy done,' Gaelene slid in loyally.

Jocasta thanked her with a quick smile, then looked appropriately repentant.

'I'm sorry,' she said.

'Make sure it doesn't happen again,' Christian instructed, and, in blistering detail, proceeded to relate how, among other errors, she had mispronounced a place name and laughed at a joke a beat too soon. She squirmed. He had not missed a thing. 'When this is over, I'd like you to stay,' he said, as his critique eventually drew to a close. 'There's a location assignment we need to discuss.'

Despite his censure and despite the morning's calamities, all of a sudden Jocasta found it difficult to keep from grinning. At long last her worth had been recognised and he was now willing to grant her equal status with the other presenters. Alleluia! A location assignment—what could it be? she wondered, as another victim was metaphorically strapped to a chair and positioned beneath the director's bare light bulb. Excitedly, she ran through a mental list of imminent events which had been gathered from the newspapers and the teletyped stream of information which TKFM received. It seemed unlikely he would send her scooting across state on her first time out, but tomorrow a group of congressmen were visiting New Orleans and would be touring the port. A controversial fraud trial loomed. A winner of the Nobel prize for literature, an Englishman, had checked into one of the city's skyscraper hotels, because he planned to set his next book in 'the Big Easy'. The grin escaped. Of course, as a fellow Brit, she would be interviewing the author.

In time, the explanations and reprimands came to an end and the room emptied. Christian asked if she would care for another cup of coffee, and when Jocasta shook her head he went over to the sideboard and poured one out for himself.

'How much do you know about alligators?' he enquired, coming back to sit opposite her across the table.

Puzzled, Jocasta looked at him. Was this some kind of trick question? Or the start of a joke? Could he be about to embark on an anecdote before they settled down to business?

'Nothing,' she replied. 'Why?'

'Because there's a farmer who has one which he reckons is lovesick. Apparently the family keep it as a pet, and it lives in luxury; swims in their pool, is fed specially prepared meals, gets taken for walks daily.'

'You want me to do a story on that?' Jocasta asked, her enthusiasm crashing down to ground-level with a deadening bump.

Christian nodded. 'For St Valentine's Day. We usually sign off with an amusing tail-piece——' for the first time that morning, the Michelangelo lips curved '—and Al the alligator languishing for lack of love sounds perfect.'

She floundered and for a moment was tempted to laugh, then a jolt of anger overtook her. She had uprooted herself from family and friends; she had risked swapping an undeniably good job for one which, although it was a once-in-a-lifetime chance, had been something of an unknown quantity; she had marked time for an entire month, and for what—to be tossed a couple of minutes of froth? Big deal! The implacability of his grey eyes had warned that Christian McCoid was the kind of man you messed with at your peril and so, despite orchestrating a number of fantasy discussions, whenever she had faced him in the flesh she had remained subdued and silent. Jocasta straightened. She would be neither subdued nor silent any longer.

'No, thank you,' she replied.

'The alligator's domesticated.'

'I don't care if it wears an apron and runs round with a vacuum cleaner,' she said. 'If you don't mind, I'll pass.'

A muscle tightened in the firm jaw. Clearly his minions were not in the habit of rejecting assignments and, clearly, he *did* mind.

'You have an aversion to animals?' Christian enquired, tugging at his tie with impatient fingers and loosening the knot.

'I have an aversion to loony fillers!'

'The viewers like them.'

'Maybe, and I've totalled up my quota in my time. However, now——'

'Now you consider yourself too much of a class act?' he suggested.

Jocasta's full mouth thinned. In both the local press and letters from viewers there had been so many references to her having 'class' and being 'classy' that she had grown heartily sick of the description. Especially when, in reality, all anyone meant was that instead of a southern-belle drawl she spoke with a clear English accent.

'I consider I'm capable of something more demanding than acting as straight man to a reptile,' she retorted.

'Look, honey,' Christian said, in a voice which although soft contained a warning core of steel, 'Max Baumgarten may have installed you, but where programme planning's concerned I'm the boss. And, should you be tempted to run and complain, please be assured that when it comes to the crunch it'll be my wishes Max will respect.'

Although Jocasta had not the least intention of whinging to the television company's millionaire proprietor, there could be no doubt Christian spoke the truth. Under pressure or not, over the past month she had recognised him to be incisive, adroit and imaginative. A man whose instincts were artistic while his output was commercial, he was one of television's movers and shakers. Mr Baumgarten appreciated his merits, and his value, too. Hadn't he said that the three television giants of ABC, CBS and NBC had each offered enticing contracts, and how fortunate it was for TKFM that the director had chosen to stay in New Orleans?

'I won't be complaining to him,' Jocasta replied, and took a breath. 'However, I am complaining to you.'

'Don't. If I ask you to interview a guy with an alligator, you interview him. *Comprendi?*'

She sighed. 'Perfectly,' she said.

'An appointment's been made for two this afternoon. Chip's your cameraman and Ed'll cover sound. Liaise with them.'

'Will do.' Jocasta's chin lifted. 'A British writer's in town to——'

'Gaelene's seeing him tomorrow.'

'Gaelene?' she repeated uncertainly.

The black girl was a bubbly and likeable personality, but she had confessed to a lack of interest in the more serious subjects and, in consequence, sometimes shirked her homework. When this happened, she would skim across the surface and neglect to ask those penetrating yet often wonderfully rewarding questions. But the writer was a feisty intellectual whose long and chequered life could, if properly mined, offer up a wealth of fascinating information.

Christian downed a mouthful of coffee. 'You don't approve?'

'I think—um, perhaps Barton would be better,' she said, reluctant to voice doubts about the colleague who had so swiftly shown herself to be a friend.

'So do I,' he agreed briefly. 'However, tomorrow is the only time the guy's willing to talk and Barton's up-state for another day.'

Jocasta shone her most appealing smile, the one which had bewitched government min-

isters and captains of industry and other lu-
minaries and made them desperate to comply
with her wishes.

'Couldn't I interview the writer?' she
enquired.

Christian shook his head. 'No.'

'Why not?'

'Because I care about *First Watch*—care
deeply—and I'm not in the business of taking
chances with a new girl. You serve your ap-
prenticeship, and in the meantime——' the pale
grey eyes seared like a blow torch '—you don't
push!'

Jocasta gave a strangled laugh. 'Push?' she
protested, 'I consider I'm being amazingly re-
strained. Grief, I've been here for a month and
never——'

'A month isn't long,' he cut in.

'It might not seem so to you, but it does to
me!' she flared, then a divining rod crease appeared between her brows. Now that their imagined conversation had become reality, instead
of locking horns she would do better, Jocasta
realised, to seize the moment and try to defuse
his hostility. 'I'm aware there's a group of
people who are fans of Debra Ellaice and who
would have preferred her to have stayed on and
obviously you're one of them,' she said, in an
abrupt change of tack. 'I'm sorry about that,

but I didn't apply to join the programme, nor
did I realise my inclusion would be at the expense of her being ditched.' She hesitated.
'Gaelene said Debra's still holed up at her sis-
ter's house in Baton Rouge, where she's become
something of a recluse.'

'That's correct.' A pulse beat in Christian's
temple. 'She isn't interested in a different job
with TKFM nor in another job in television,
come to that.'

'She's had offers?'

'A couple of other networks have made ap-
proaches. However, all Debra wants is to be
left alone, or so she informed my answering
machine yesterday evening.'

'She must be very hurt,' Jocasta noted
ruefully.

'With a vengeance,' he muttered.

Her heart sank. To know she had caused
such grief, albeit unwittingly, was not pleasant.
'Hurt, but overreacting,' she defended.
'Debra's dismissal sounds to have been most
abrupt, so she has just reason to feel slighted,
but I don't understand why she needed to rush
away from New Orleans a month ago. And
now—well, coming on like Greta Garbo is too
emotional, too hysterical, too extreme.'

Christian nipped his fingers to the bridge of
his nose in a gesture of weariness, and, for a

moment, closed his eyes. Could he be suffering from lack of sleep, too?

'Your response would have been different?' he asked.

'I'd have fought,' Jocasta acknowledged. 'I feel bad about Debra,' she continued, 'but——'

'But you can't help it if you're thirteen years younger?'

'No.'

'And easier on the eye?'

She shot him a look. Spoken with a gentler inflexion, this could have been a compliment; instead it sounded like a slur.

'Maybe,' Jocasta agreed cautiously.

'Neither can you help it if you're a darn sight hungrier?' Christian enquired.

Her hackles rose. Why must he persist in turning what anyone else would regard as assets into liabilities?

'You consider ambition to be a dirty word?' she questioned.

'On the contrary, I applaud ambition—so long as it's kept within reasonable limits.'

'And mine isn't?' she demanded, for the implication seemed to be that in coming to New Orleans and taking Debra's place she had shown herself to be a hard-nosed and ruthless little madam.

Christian moved broad shoulders. 'You know the answer to that one, not me.'

'Yes, I do, and——' Stricken by guilt and sudden unwelcome memories, Jocasta brought herself up short.

'Having doubts?' he murmured.

Her thoughts were shuffled aside. 'None,' she declared stoutly. 'Maybe undertaking a job-change which also involves a change of country is rare, but it isn't unique. Far from it. You may choose to stick to New Orleans——'

'And be a stick-in-the-mud?' Christian enquired, with the arch of a brow. 'Wrong. I've also worked abroad, on current affairs programmes in France for close to five years. And, for the record, I was partly educated there, too.'

Gaelene's gossip had not stretched this far and the information came as a surprise, but everything fitted. Now she understood his European-style sophistication, the dexterity of his television touch, and why his southern accent was not only diluted, but possessed an intriguingly intricate difference.

'So your ambition was responsible for *you* travelling thousands of miles!' Jocasta said, with an exultant smile.

'It wasn't the same,' he rejected curtly.

'You mean you're not female.' She gave an exasperated sigh. 'OK, for a woman of my age to job-hop in the way I've done is unusual, but ambition was not the only reason for my leaving England. As a matter of fact——' On the brink of revealing a second, deeply personal motivation, she changed her mind. This was not the time or place for true confessions. 'Um— I like to travel and while I'm here I hope to fit in lots of sightseeing. If you put your prejudice aside for a moment, you'd see that in having me sit on the sofa and make small talk for ever and a day you're under-utilising me,' Jocasta carried on determinedly. 'I have a brain. I'm well read. I keep cool under stress. I can handle the high-calibre subjects, like politics, the environment, ethical issues.'

Christian tipped back his chair and linked his hands behind his head. 'So—the message is that the girl who's been wheeled in as the resident bimbo actually thinks like a professor?'

Jocasta's eyes chilled to iceberg-blue. One of the greatest and most repetitive difficulties she had encountered in her work was preconception. Because she possessed a mane of long fair hair, a good complexion and went in and out at all the right places, there was a tendency among some people to assume she could not be very bright. Attractiveness had its drawbacks. Granted, there were advantages, too—

a well-timed smile could perform wonders—but she had refused to trade on her looks and had resolutely based her career on efficiency, determination and old-fashioned hard slog. Her efforts had paid dividends, for she was good at what she did!

'A professor who can do joined-up writing,' she retaliated, with spirit. 'I'm not a bimbo and I wasn't brought in as such. I may be twenty-seven and blonde, but Mr Baumgarten knows I'm proficient at my job. Extremely proficient.'

'You reckon Max is a shrewd judge when it comes to staff selection?' Christian demanded, in what sounded suspiciously like a loaded question.

Her brow puckered. In all honesty, she had no idea. Yet, as well as his communications companies, the man who had been so anxious to enlist her services ran a top-notch building firm and owned vast tracts of property—so he could not be short on grey matter.

'I reckon he knows what's good for TKFM,' she replied, then continued, 'I have an excellent track record, as you must have gathered from my videos, and——'

'Which videos?' Christian cut in.

'The ones I provided giving examples of my previous work. Hasn't Mr Baumgarten passed them on?'

'I've received nothing.'

Jocasta frowned. If he had not seen what she had done, then it explained his reluctance to allot her more worthwhile assignments—to a degree.

'That's odd,' she said, recalling how their overlord, a somewhat gruff individual, had swooped on her tapes and enthused over them at length. 'He must have forgotten. I'll ask him to let you have them. But Mr Baumgarten must have told you about my work,' she persisted.

Christian swallowed down the remains of his coffee. 'The guy waxed poetical.'

'If ageism and sexism reign supreme in television in the States, don't blame me,' Jocasta said, irked by his sarcasm.

'Sexism?' he queried.

'I haven't heard any talk of Barton being replaced, so presumably men are considered watchable even when they pass the dreaded fortieth birthday. However,' she went on, 'apart from her reaching what Mr Baumgarten appears to have considered the end of her shelf-life, I understand that for several months before her dismissal Debra had been becoming increasingly distracted.'

With a single clench of a large fist, Christian crushed his paper cup. 'Claptrap,' he bit out.

'She also had an inclination to coast, and was a little dull and middle-of-the-road.' Jocasta shone a sweet smile. 'But we all know what happens if you stay in the middle—you get run over.' She had never met the older woman and if she did would offer sincere sympathy at her fate, but his 'bimbo' gibe had cut deep. It wounded. It offended. It also made it essential she hammer home the point that her arrival on the scene represented an all-round improvement. 'Let me interview the writer and you'll see that I don't coast. Ever. I give one hundred per cent. I——'

'What's all the hurry?' he cut in.

'Couldn't you let me do just one piece which demands more than nods of the head or merry quips?' she pleaded.

'In time,' Christian said tersely.

'How much time?'

'Maybe in another month or two.'

'Another month or two?' Jocasta protested, her voice rising in horror.

The paper cup described a perfect arc as he tossed it into the waste-paper basket. 'Patience is a virtue,' he quoted.

'So I've heard,' she replied grimly. For a moment she was silent, thinking about the four weeks—or eight!—which stretched out before her like a gaol sentence, then she squared her shoulders. 'Although I'm versatile, adding another spoonful of sugar to the diet of breakfast television is not really my style,' Jocasta told him, deciding she might as well air all the grievances which had been simmering. 'Being relentlessly jolly at such an hour doesn't come easy. In fact, it's agony,' she found herself saying a touch melodramatically, as she warmed to her theme.

'Then why did you take the *First Watch* job?'

She sighed. 'Because Mr Baumgarten steam-rollered me, but I never realised what a strain perpetual early starts would be. I hate going to bed before ten, and as for getting up at dawn it's——'

'You're breaking my heart,' Christian interrupted. 'However, I can think of one solution.'

'Which is?'

'To tender your resignation.'

Jocasta ignored him. 'I'd be far better suited to something meatier,' she declared.

'You want to switch to another programme?' he asked, with a look which said she must be out of her mind.

'Please. The evening news programme would be ideal.'

Christian uttered a disparaging oath. 'I'm aware of the edict which says if you don't believe in yourself no one else will, but in making a bid for prime time——'

'All I want is to carve a decent niche for myself.'

'—your expectations are a little high. Indeed, the only way you'll appear on the evening show is if you chloroform me first!' he rasped, and rising from the table he strode over to the window, where he pushed his hands into the pockets of his jeans and stared out at the wide, slow-moving waters of the Mississippi.

A taut silence followed, during which Jocasta wondered why he was so against her. Christian might not have seen her videos, but he had seen her in action, and although the jobs tackled had been of the tuppenny-ha'penny variety— thanks to him—she considered she had acquitted herself well. Should she promote her redeployment again? Could he, somehow, be persuaded? Warily, she eyed the rigid set of his shoulders. No, at this point settling for an expanded role in *First Watch* seemed to be more politic. Still, no matter how much the early rising rankled, remaining *in situ* was a long way from the death of a thousand cuts, Jocasta comforted herself. In America the good breakfast programmes came second in prestige to the evening telecasts and, unlike their British equivalents, played an important part in the

national news agenda. Her mind went to the
tapes she had watched of her predecessor on
air. With a silver-blonde metallic bob and ha-
bitually wearing pearls over highly coloured
jerseys, Debra Ellaice had handled her fair
share of the topical items.

'As I've taken over from Debra, shouldn't I
cover the kind of assignments she would have
covered?' Jocasta suggested tentatively.

Christian swivelled from the window to
glower. 'You want me to chisel it on a tablet
of stone?' he demanded. 'Slow down.'

'But——'

'To use a four-letter word—*wait,*' he rasped,
then frowned as a knock sounded on the door.
'Come in.'

One of the receptionists from the desk in the
main entrance hall had arrived, carrying a
bouquet of lilies, carnations and roses.
Wrapped in cellophane and tied with a scarlet
bow, the bouquet was as splendid as those
which were presented to prima donnas in grand
opera houses.

'I'm looking for Jocasta,' the girl explained,
and grinned at her. 'These have been delivered
for you.'

She received the flowers with thanks and
surprise, and as the receptionist left she opened

the white envelope which was pinned to the ribbon and took out a card.

'From a secret admirer,' Jocasta read, and wrinkled her nose. 'I would who it is?'

'You're telling me you don't know?' Christian protested. 'I'd say it's a guy who has plenty of money. Or one who thinks a lot of you. Or both.' He thrust her a piercing glance. 'Ring any bells?'

'None.' The bouquet was laid down on the table. 'I believe a demographics forecast showed that if changes weren't made *First Watch* could have been in danger of losing some of the younger viewers which the advertisers demand,' Jocasta said, in a last-ditch attempt at her campaign for a more substantial workload, 'and already TKFM's received letters which indicate that people, young and old, like me. The general consensus seems to be that I'm doing a good job, and——' she took a blip of breath '— I'd do an even better one if you'd let me.'

Picking up the flowers, Christian bundled them into her arms, then strode forward and opened wide the door.

'Goodbye,' he said.

'What do I have to do, go down on my knees?' Jocasta protested. 'When Mr Baumgarten hired me——'

'But why did he hire *you?*' he interjected. 'What made him bring you all this way when we have plenty of young, pretty——'

'Bimbos?' she slid in astringently.

'——female television presenters of our own?'

'I'm in America because, in addition to being able to do everything they can do—and do it well,' she emphasised, 'I have a different accent. One which people like.'

'That right? Two o'clock appointment. Don't forget,' Christian instructed.

Jocasta gave him a look which could have cut through concrete. 'I won't,' she said, and marched out into the corridor.

# CHAPTER TWO

SUPPLANTING Debra Ellaice might not have have been her fault, but it was her problem, Jocasta brooded, as she waited for the 'walk' sign to show. However, the minute she arrived home she would ring Mr Baumgarten's office again—when she had called from the studios he had been in a meeting—and request that her videos be handed over. Soonest. Once Christian McCoid had seen them, he would realise that she had amassed a moderately distinguished body of work, his attitude would undergo an obliging change, and...

Icy humid air was shearing off the Mississippi, and the wind snatching at the bouquet forced her to tighten her grip. Jocasta shivered. She had heard many tales of New Orleans' steamy summer heat, but no one had said how cold it could be in winter. At last she was able to cross the road and leave the wind-swept avenue of Canal Street for the narrow, more protected by-ways of the French Quarter. As she walked along, her mouth spread into a smile. Even in the cold weather, tourists flocked to the Vieux Carré or 'Old Square' in their hundreds, and she understood why. A self-contained area of seven by thirteen blocks, the French Quarter, with its prettily balconied houses and lush hidden courtyards were a charming reminder of the city's pot-pourri ethnic heritage—Spanish, French, Indian, and many others. Here there were art galleries and antique shops by the dozen, museums, boutiques, restaurants. And music, music, music. It was in the evening when the jazz clubs came alive, but although it had yet to reach noon Dixieland trumpet sounds were wafting from doorways and street-corner entertainers had begun to gather the crowds. Jocasta passed a little black boy and his grandfather tap-dancing to the strains of a cassette recorder, then a girl plucking at a banjo, then a kerbside honky-tonk piano player. Her smile widened. The French Quarter was fun and, courtesy of the house building firm which formed the nub of Mr Baumgarten's business empire, she was lucky enough to live here. Her employment package had included a two-bedroomed town-house in a tucked-away development of four, which had been sympathetically designed to blend into the old-world surroundings.

'How ya doin', Jo?' a voice hollered, and she looked across the street.

Her television exposure meant Jocasta had already begun to be recognised. Sometimes strangers would yodel a hello, but now the owner of a Creole bistro was waving. A man of ample girth and ready smile, like so many of her neighbours he had been warm and welcoming.

'I'm fine, Alex,' she called.

'*First Watch* is usually too early for me, but I caught a glimpse this morning and, gee, are you giving the programme a kick in the rear.'

'Thanks,' she said, and they enjoyed a short, shouted conversation.

Minutes later, when she visited a bookstore, the owner greeted her like a long-lost friend, and as she turned into the cobbled alleyway which led down to her townhouse someone else carolled a 'Have a nice day'. Jocasta grinned. New Orleans might be a big city, but the French Quarter possessed all the friendliness of a small town.

Once indoors she went straight to the telephone, but on punching out his office number was now informed that Mr Baumgarten had left for home. And when she rang his grand antebellum villa in the city's Garden District, the housekeeper said he had gone out.

'He's buying some last-minute purchases for his cruise,' the woman explained. 'Not taken a vacation in years, but at the weekend he picks up a brochure for a liner which sails around the world and—what d'you know?—he decides to go.'

Jocasta raised her brows. The middle-aged divorcé had seemed ill at ease with socialising and she was surprised he should choose such a communal all-friends-together type of holiday. But she did not know him well. Indeed, in England she had spent just a few hours in his company, and since her arrival their contact had been limited to a single phone call when he had rung to ask if she was satisfied with her accommodation. She might be his protégée, but Max Baumgarten had not bothered to introduce her to her colleagues, nor looked into the studio to check on how she was adapting. When she had commented on this lack of interest, Gaelene had said it was typical. The owner of TKFM preferred to concentrate on his building company and, apart from the occasional out-of-the-blue demand or suggestion, left the running of his television and radio stations in the hands of the professionals.

'How long will Mr Baumgarten be away?' she enquired.

'Three months. How he can desert his office on the spur of the moment and for that length of time, don't ask me,' the housekeeper said, astonishment at her employer's decision provoking a need to talk. Her tone dropped into confidentiality. 'Though to be honest, he's always been a bit erratic and it's become worse since his wife walked out. Left him a few years ago without warning and took their daughter with her. He was devoted to that girl.' There was a noisy sigh. 'Mr B's off first thing in the morning.'

'I'd be grateful if he could pass on some videos before he goes,' Jocasta said, and explained.

'Leave it with me. I'll have a word and see Mr McCoid gets them,' the woman assured her. 'Bye.'

As Jocasta located vases and began to dismantle the bouquet, she frowned. She had told Christian that the decisive factor in why Max Baumgarten had hired her was her accent and yet, on reflection, he had paid little attention to the way she spoke. Indeed, after one passing reference her pronunciation had been ignored. So what had so impressed him that a chance look at television during a European business trip had had him ringing the studios, arranging a meeting, insisting she must join his network? The walrus-moustachioed Louisianan had remarked on what he had called her 'poised yet gutsy manner', but was there an additional appeal? The carnations' lower leaves were stripped clean. It did not matter. All that mattered was that she was here.

Here, and eager to make her mark. But was she too eager, as Christian had insisted? Could she be suffering from that career 'tunnel vision' which had caused so much heartbreak before, and had this created an unrealistic timescale? Was she still attempting to climb the ladder three rungs at a stride? Making a clear-eyed assessment of yourself could be tricky, but after searching her conscience Jocasta was sure the answer came in the negative. Nevertheless, keeping her aspirations chained up for another month would be frustrating. Though Christian had only said that after a month or two *maybe* he would sanction her progress, she recalled, as she started arranging the blooms. Plus, he had suggested she could leave. Dismay gripped, like fingers tight around her throat. On consideration, both comments seemed ominous. Did the news director possess genuine doubts about her capabilities—doubts which her videos must lay to rest—or might he be deliberately restricting her in the hope that, before too long, she would become fed up and go? Had the arbitrary manner in which she had been foisted on him generated a determination to ignore her talents, come what may? Christian did not strike her as a vindictive kind of man, and yet . . . Dejection seeped in. Jocasta shied away from painting worst-case scenarios, but if a definite decision had been made to limit her, then the videos were not going to make one scrap of difference, and what had seemed a dazzling career move could turn out to be a doomed endeavour.

She stiffened her spine. Failure was out of the question. If the sight of her visual curriculum vitae did not do the trick, then she would need to find some other way of persuading Christian McCoid that she must be allowed to progress. A dark red rosebud was added to one of the white ceramic flutes. She would need to cancel out his image of her as an elbowing upstart. She would need to win him over. She would need to perform television magic and thus force him to acknowledge—and use—her expertise. Though what kind of magic, she did not know.

The vases were placed around the open-plan living-room, then she prepared herself an early lunch. As she ate the broccoli quiche and green salad, Jocasta opened the book she had bought and began to read. Time was passing. Soon the camera crew would be collecting her, but before then there was information to glean. Her head down, she was working hard when the telephone on the bureau rang. With a sigh she went to answer it.

'Good afternoon,' she said, and gave the number.

Silence.

'Jocasta Chater speaking,' she said, wondering if this might be Chip calling to warn her that he and Ed were going to be late.

Again silence. Her brow creased. She was sure there was somebody at the other end of the wire. She could not explain why, she just knew.

'Good afternoon,' Jocasta repeated, and heard a gruff masculine sound which was not quite a grunt, not quite an intake of breath, but which confirmed her intuition. 'Who is this?' she demanded.

When there was no reply, unease formed a knot in the pit of her stomach. To know someone was there, someone who had heard her but who refused to answer, felt scary and unsettling. It might be broad daylight and whoever it was had said nothing, but ... She shuddered. Once she had been involved in a TV programme about men who were addicted to making nuisance calls, and now she wondered whether her caller had rung at random or because he knew she lived here? He couldn't know. Her name was not in the book and only the TKFM staff had access to her number. The knot tightened. But he knew now, she realised, because she had told him.

'Buzz off,' Jocasta said incisively, and slammed down the receiver.

A telephone pest made an apt addition to the day, she thought ruefully as she resumed her reading, but—fingers crossed—it would be the last of the mishaps, disappointments and general trouble.

It wasn't.

A couple of afternoons later, Jocasta was alone in the presenters' room when the door opened and Christian looked in.

'Any idea where I can find Barton?' he asked.

She broke off from sifting through a collection of newspaper cuttings. 'His throat's sore so he's gone out to buy medicine, but he should be back soon.'

'I've run your piece of film, and for someone who reckoned to know zilch about alligators you managed to slide in a remarkable number of facts,' he said, walking forward. 'I had no idea there were around half a million in the Louisiana swamplands, nor that, while the females don't normally exceed ten feet, males can grow to as much as twenty.' He gave a low whistle. 'Some size. The story's too good to use as a tailpiece so I've decided to include it as a feature. We'll show it at the beginning of next week, probably Tuesday.'

Jocasta beamed. 'Thank you.'

Loony filler or not, she had approached the assignment with her usual dedication and now she wanted to cheer. He liked what she had done. Christian *approved*. All of a sudden it felt as if it was Christmas and her birthday, rolled into one.

'However, I have a criticism,' he added.

Her delight dissolved into a silent groan. So much for hip-hip-hooray! She should have guessed his pat on the back would come swiftly followed by a blow to the head.

'Which is?' Jocasta enquired.

'The film ended too abruptly.' The presenters' room was used by a stream of people from different programmes, and Christian needed to push aside a mound of papers, ashtrays and personal debris in order to rest a hip on the corner of the desk. 'You gave me the required footage—just—but I'd have welcomed a lingering shot of you, the farmer and——' a brow twitched '—Al? to round off the sequence.'

'I'd have liked that, too. But lingering is the last thing on your mind when a creature with twenty pairs of teeth in each jaw decides you're the answer to his prayers,' Jocasta said succinctly.

A small smile seeded itself at the corner of his mouth. 'Tell me,' he instructed.

She sighed. 'At the end of the shoot, we returned to the farmyard where I stood with Al and the farmer to do a closing "piece to camera",' she explained. 'As I was talking I felt a nudge and realised Al had begun stroking my foot, but I managed to ignore it. With difficulty.' She flinched at the memory. 'However, seconds later he began making low soft noises which, when combined with stroking, can be a prelude to mating, according to the book I'd read. So I decided on a hasty retreat!'

'You were courted by an alligator?' Christian said, and started to laugh.

'It was no joke,' Jocasta protested, but a smile spread and suddenly she was laughing, too.

At the time the incident had caused total terror, but now she saw the funny side. And Christian's amusement was infectious. With his eyes crinkled at the corners and uninhibited chuckles coming from him, he was so different from the critical fault-finder.

'But the farmer had Al on a strong chain,' he said.

'Only until I walked away.'

His mirth switched off. 'And then?'

'Al broke the chain, like a thread. He might have been tame, but he was wild for a mate. Up until then I'd been the Queen of Cool,' Jocasta told him, in cheerful self-mockery, 'but at that point my walking switched to a run. Well, when I say run, it was actually a frantic totter in my high heels—with him making chase.'

'Oh, hell!' Christian exclaimed, laughing again.

'Alligators are supposed to lie torpid during the winter season, but could he move fast! However, as luck would have it, ahead of me was a walled pen so, moving into my Olympic-high-jump-champion mode, I made a leap for it.' Her hand sketched a soaring bound. 'Whee—clunk.'

'Clunk?'

'I got stuck halfway. However, I huffed and I puffed,' she said jokily, 'and eventually managed to tumble over the side to safety.'

'You weren't hurt?' he demanded.

'No, but I landed in a load of... manure.' She rolled her eyes. 'Not to be recommended.'

He grinned. 'I can imagine.'

Jocasta located a folder from among the jumble on the desk and handed him an expense claim form. 'Please could you initial this before I pass it through to Accounts?'

'One sweater,' Christian read. 'One skirt. One pair of stockings. One pair of shoes.'

'All ruined.'

'And I hoped that clip would be cheap,' he muttered. His eyes moved down the sheet. 'One white lace bra.'

'The manure soaked in,' she explained.

'Can't it be washed out?'

'No.'

'So what have you done with your bra?'

Jocasta bridled. The only reason she had been chased and covered in dung was in order to provide *him* with a story, and now he was questioning her claim? How dared he? Others might doctor their expenses, but she never had and she strongly objected to this interrogation.

An ice-bright smile was dispensed. 'I burnt it—of course.'

'One pair of briefs. One suspender belt,' he continued, and she detected a flicker of curiosity. Presumably the women of his acquaintance wore tights.

'A suspender belt is a contraption which fastens around the hips. Made of white satin and lace, in this case,' she informed him sassily. 'At intervals there are suspenders which——'

'Thanks, but I do have a working knowledge of female underwear,' Christian intervened brusquely. 'And yours was beyond redemption?'

'Completely. I needed to buy a whole new set.' Jocasta's fingers went to the neck of her black jumpsuit. 'I can supply the receipts, but perhaps you'd prefer it if I showed you?'

His eyes met hers in a level look. 'Why not?' he said.

Her heart beat erratically. Her pulse started to race. The question had been asked facetiously in angry defiance and with the full expectation that he would shrug and say not to bother, he would take her word for it. Instead, Christian had issued a challenge. Did she meet it, or did she back away? For a moment Jocasta stared into the depths of his grey eyes, then she hooked a rebellious finger into the ring at the top of the zip which went from collar to elasticated waist to thigh-level. She would show him she was a woman to be reckoned with. She would call his bluff. As she pulled the ring downwards, all other noise seemed to cease. Common sense insisted the hustle bustle of the studios must still be circulating around them, yet the muted brrr of the zip seemed to be the only sound in the room, in the building, in the world. Down the zip went. Slowly down, revealing her throat, her chest and the first swelling of her breasts. Jocasta looked at him. He looked steadily back. Christian would lose his nerve and call a halt. He must, she begged silently. Please. Now.

His eyes fell to the smooth-skinned curves which were being tantalisingly revealed, then reluctantly, yet compulsively and with naked masculine interest, lurched down to her slender waist, to the roundness of her hips, and up again until, once more, he met her gaze. Was he wondering if she was wearing a suspender belt now? Could he be imagining her lacy underwear? Aware of mixed signals, Jocasta frowned. One half of Christian McCoid might resent her presence, but the other half was responding to her as a slim, curvy and sexually appealing woman. As his eyes tangled with hers, the emotional temperature rose and the space between them seemed to sizzle. It was crazy, she knew, but at the stroke of his gaze over her body the points of her breasts had tightened and now her skin felt hot and tender.

Jocasta's fingers shook, fumbled, yet she continued to pull. She would not give in. No. No. No. Her heart thumped *fortissimo*. The silence grew heavier, the sound of the zip louder. Her bra, which was low cut and in full view, now seemed to diminish to brazenly wanton proportions.

'How long have you been attending how-to-flirt classes?' Christian demanded, all of a sudden.

Her trembling hand halted. 'Pardon me?'

Sweeping from the desk, he folded his arms and stood with long legs set apart. His stance was aggressive and his face as black as thunder.

'If this is an exercise in seduction, you've come to the wrong man,' he scythed. 'My name isn't Max Baumgarten.'

Jocasta hastily tugged the zip up to her neck. 'Max Baumgarten?' she queried.

'You may have turned him into the proverbial putty, but——'

'Putty? You mean you think I've seduced him? You think that's—that's why he employed me?' she protested, spluttering in her indignation. 'You think I'm here courtesy of—of casting-couch tactics? Grief, Mr Baumgarten's old enough to be my father.'

'So?'

'So you're insane!'

Silence.

'To get back to your performance just now,' Christian said grittily. 'A striptease is a little *too* obvious.'

'It was not a striptease and I can assure you I was not trying to seduce you!' she blazed.

'Then what the hell were you doing?'

Jocasta looked at him. It was a good question. What had she been doing? Where did this unsuspected exhibitionism come from? Why, instead of acting like the air-headed tootsie he believed her to be, hadn't she met his challenge with regal disdain? She was attempting to think of the answer, any answer, when the telephone on the desk suddenly shrilled.

'Jocasta Chater here,' she gabbled, snatching it up as a heaven-sent diversion.

'There's a man on the line who refuses to give his name, but who reckons he's your most ardent follower,' the telephonist told her. 'I'm connecting you.'

There was the usual click. 'Good morning,' she said. No answer. 'Jocasta Chater here,' she repeated. Still nothing. 'Hello?' When Christian shifted impatiently, she placed her hand over the mouthpiece and told him what the telephonist had said, but that there was a delay. 'Perhaps he's the person who sent the flowers,' she speculated, as the silence continued.

Christian frowned. 'The guy still hasn't identified himself?'

'No, and as my social life is non-existent—not too many invitations come your way when you're restricted to a ten p.m. curfew,' Jocasta said, in a pert reminder, 'who else could have sent them but a fan?'

'Must be an extreme type.'

'The word "fan" is derived from "fanatic",' she pointed out, and flashed the switchboard. 'The girl insists we're connected.'

'Maybe the prospect of speaking to his dream girl is so mind-blowing he's become tongue-tied,' Christian suggested laconically.

Tempted to hit him—hard—instead she concentrated on the call.

'Jocasta Chater,' she enunciated again.

He bent forward. 'Your friendly neighbourhood striptease artist,' he murmured.

Unsure whether this was more condemnation or if he might now be joking, she darted him a glance—but his expression was cool and unreadable. Hearing a noise, Jocasta listened, then she frowned and replaced the receiver.

'Odd,' she said. 'When you spoke, whoever it was gave a grunt and ended the call. Someone rang my home number a couple of days ago and they didn't speak either, they just sort of grunted.'

'It would have been a wrong number.'

'Probably,' she agreed for, when she had thought about it later, to interpret silence as a nuisance call did seem far-fetched. 'You've seen the alligator film, so have you also had a chance to look at my videos?' Jocasta enquired.

The intention had been to keep her mouth firmly buttoned and wait until *he* mentioned them, but now she was leery of their conversation reverting to the expenses claim et cetera. Especially the et cetera. If he gave permission for her to be reimbursed, fine. If not, she would not be arguing the case a second time.

Christian shook his head. 'They haven't arrived.'

'No? When I rang Mr Baumgarten was preparing to go on holiday, but his housekeeper promised to tell him.'

'She did. She called earlier to say she realised it must have slipped his mind and she'd been searching for the tapes, but without success.' He shrugged. 'I'll screen them when Max gets back.'

Jocasta glared, irritated by this nonchalant dismissal. So much hinged on him seeing her videos and seeing them *soon*.

'And what happens in the meantime?' she demanded. 'I'm to inhabit that damned sofa and talk sweet nothings for the next three months?'

'I know plenty of presenters who would give their right arms to "inhabit that damned sofa",' Christian told her silkily.

She frowned. What he said was true, and if she grumbled too much he might well resurrect the suggestion that she quit. And could attempt to enforce it!

'Do you think the housekeeper knows which tapes they are?' Jocasta asked.

'Yes. She said she'd seen Max watching them, but now they've disappeared. She thinks they could be in his safe, but she doesn't have the combination.'

'Why would he have put them in a safe?' Jocasta protested. 'If the housekeeper looks again I'm sure she'll find them.'

'Are you? I'm not. They could be under lock and key, or Max may even have taken the tapes on his cruise with him. Anything is possible,' Christian said, when she began to object. 'The big enchilada may be smart when it comes to making money, but he can do things which are downright eccentric. For example, once he had a pond dug in his backyard. It was damn near swimming-pool size and surrounded with granite boulders which were specially brought in. Max stocked it with rare and expensive fish. Then six weeks later he decides he prefers lawn. So the fish were removed, the hole filled——'

'The housekeeper said he could be quirky,' she cut in impatiently, and returned to what mattered. 'There are copies of my videos back home. My parents are away visiting friends, but as soon as they return I'll ring my mother and ask her to send them over airmail.'

'Up to you.' Christian checked the steel and brass watch fastened to his wrist. 'There's a story I'd like you to do on termites——' a brow lifted '——unless you have some objection?'

She gritted her teeth. 'None.'

'Glory be! Termites are an increasing problem in New Orleans and particularly in the French Quarter,' he said, gathering speed. 'A number of residents have banded together in order to——'

'I've read about it,' Jocasta said.

'Fine. What I have in mind is a film coupled with a studio interview, the whole thing to fit a ten-minute slot. There's no urgency, but I'd be obliged if you'd get your spade and start digging.'

'How about the termite story being incorporated into, say, half a dozen short films featuring French Quarter buildings?' she enquired, as he strode towards the door.

Christian halted in his tracks and turned. 'You want to do a series?' he demanded.

She nodded, then glanced at the newspaper cuttings which were spread on the desk. 'I'd also like to arrange to——'

His grey eyes darkened to gunmetal. 'Back off,' he ordered.

'In the past I didn't hang around waiting to be offered assignments, I often rooted them out for myself. And the other presenters here cover stories which they've found,' Jocasta protested.

Christian inspected his watch again. 'I'm strapped for time. Stick with the termites. *Please.*'

'There are some fascinating houses in the French Quarter, each with its own fascinating history,' she carried on doggedly. 'There's the one where Tennessee Williams wrote *A Streetcar Named Desire,* and the home of Marie Laveau, the voodoo queen, and——' a hand circled abundance '—masses of others. I realise they'll be familiar to you, but how many of the people who live in TKFM's area have visited them? Also as a newcomer I'd be looking at everything from a fresh angle and——'

'Put a lock on it,' he rapped, and strode out.

Jocasta gave a daggers-drawn look at the door which had banged shut behind him. Christian might have claimed to have had no time, but the truth was that he had no interest in her ideas. None. And, after risking life and limb with a lusting alligator, she had now been awarded the grand prize of a two-bit piece on insects!

'That sigh sounds as if it goes right down to your boots,' someone sympathised, and she saw Barton coming into the room.

A gracious, debonair man with blond hair silvering at the temples, he had, like Gaelene, happily accepted her as a member of the team, and before she could stop herself Jocasta began telling him how Christian seemed determined to block her progress and cramp her style.

'He reckons it's because he cares about *First Watch,*' she fretted, 'but people have said how lacklustre Debra had become and I saw it myself from the tapes, so if he cares so much I don't understand why he wanted her to remain.'

'The situation's more complicated than that,' Barton said and, removing a couple of telephone directories from a chair, he drew it close and sat down. 'Chris's a sweet guy, but when it comes to his private life he doesn't say much nor does he like anyone else talking about it— so keep this to yourself. One evening, last summer, I was driving past the condo where he lives when I spotted Debra's car parked outside. The next day I mentioned it to her and, in confidence, she confessed that she and Chris were . . . involved.'

Jocasta's eyes stretched wide. 'They were lovers?'

'Yup. I was as surprised as you are,' her colleague told her. 'Not only is he younger than her, but Debra didn't seem his type. And there was never any hint of a liaison here at the studios.'

Her mind flew back to how she had described the older woman as distracted and dull and middle-of-the-road. Now she knew why Christian had been so tense and so angry!

'Apparently their affair started a year or so after Chris came back from France, after his wife had died,' Barton went on.

'I didn't know he'd been married,' Jocasta muttered.

'What you mean is, Gaelene doesn't know,' he said, with a dry smile. 'As I explained, Chris prefers to keep his private life strictly private, though why he should be tight-lipped about having tied the knot beats me. He was married to a French girl, I heard about it because my father and his father have a mutual friend. It's difficult to work out what's happening between him and Debra now,' he went on, 'but

I wouldn't be surprised if her leaving hasn't also finished off their relationship. Certainly this business of her refusing to see anyone appears to include Chris, too.'

Jocasta cringed. It got worse and worse. She had not only bad-mouthed his lover, she had also, it seemed, inadvertently brought an end to their affair. No wonder she was an undesirable as far as Christian McCoid was concerned!

# CHAPTER THREE

JOCASTA divided her weekend between some primary research on the French Quarter series and investigating an item which she found in the newspapers. Drug-related robberies and murders had long been a problem in New Orleans, but a couple of years earlier a politician had taken a private iniative and, at substantial cost to himself, had financed a teenagers' leisure centre in one of the city's poorer areas. Here, in addition to learning how to keep fit, box, and play a number of sports, the young people were being educated about the dangers and ugliness of the drugs scene. Jocasta felt that the centre and the politician's largesse possessed all the ingredients of a heartlifting human interest story—though doubtless Christian would pour bucketfuls of cold water!

When the *First Watch* post-mortem ended on Monday morning, she remained behind in his office.

'There's something I'd like to discuss,' she told him, as he collected another cup of coffee.

'If it's the termites——'

'It isn't. You said there wasn't any rush, so although I've arranged to see the spokes-woman for the residents' action committee our appointment isn't until later in the week. What I want to talk about is an idea I have for a story.'

'The noise you hear,' Christian informed an unseen audience, 'is me tearing out my hair.'

'It'll only take five minutes.'

He thrust her an impatient look. 'You really are hell on wheels, aren't you?'

'You're not short of drive yourself,' Jocasta responded.

This appeared to strike a chord and, dropping down into the swivel chair behind his desk, he laid a foot across his knee. 'Shoot,' he said wearily.

'I was wondering how you'd feel about William LeBlanc's being interviewed for *First Watch*?' she said, and opened the folder she carried which contained newspaper cuttings and a sheaf of notes. 'He's funded a centre——'

'In the hope of alleviating the drug menace? I know. But because you're new here what *you* don't know is that William LeBlanc is anti-media. OK, it's unusual for a politician to fight shy of publicity, if not unprecedented,' Christian said, when she manifested surprise, 'but although there was a time when he'd talk, for years now LeBlanc has given only written statements to the Press and rejected all appeals to appear on television. And because he's a prominent guy in this town, I promise you TKFM has frequently appealed. Whether he was slaughtered in an interview or has developed a phobia about being filmed I can't say, but as far as getting him on screen goes, forget it. It'd be a notable coup, but LeBlanc would never agree.'

'He already has,' Jocasta said.

Christian sat back. 'What?'

'I spoke to him yesterday and he said he'd be happy to come on the programme.'

For a moment or two he was silent and frowning, then anger swept over him like a storm-cloud in fast motion. 'You took it into your head to go and see LeBlanc as a representative of *First Watch*?' he enquired, and the foot which rested across his knee began to revolve more and more violently until it lifted him upright and he strode around the desk to confront her. 'And without one word to me?'

'I saw Mr LeBlanc by chance,' Jocasta protested. Christian's passion might make him a whizz of a lover, but right now it meant his grey eyes burned and his face was tight with fury. He looked as though he would dearly like to shake her until she rattled. The folder was hugged close to her chest. She refused to be intimidated. 'Because I'd read about the centre I went to take a look, though unofficially, and as I was watching some of the kids performing on a trampoline he appeared,' she explained. 'He started to talk about how easy it is for teenagers to become hooked on drugs, and although I immediately told him I worked for TKFM Mr LeBlanc was outgoing and courteous.'

'You mean that, like Max, when he heard your accent he was won over?' Christian gibed. 'Give me a break!'

She looked coolly at him. 'I've no idea why Mr LeBlanc should have been so friendly; all I know is—he was. He did mention that the centre needs money for extra equipment, so maybe he's hoping some television exposure will speed the fund-raising.'

Christian scowled, and began pacing up and down. 'And you asked if you could interview him?' he demanded, torn between anger at her free-wheeling independence and pleasure that the politician had, at long last, consented to come on air.

'I asked if *someone* could interview him.'

He stopped dead, his grey eyes probing hers. 'You don't want to handle it?'

From first identifying the story Jocasta had been indecently eager to make it her own, but she also acknowledged that the decision as to who should speak with the politician belonged with him.

'Very much. However, if you prefer Barton I understand.'

'You do?' he queried, plainly uncertain whether or not to believe her.

She nodded. 'You know you can rely on him, whereas with me——' No more needed to be said. 'You'd rather Barton tackled the interview, wouldn't you?'

'Yes,' Christian said immediately. 'Pleasant though he may be, LeBlanc's always struck me as the kind of guy who's adroit at concealing things and if he resorted to any evasion Barton would be tougher on him than you.' He gave a thin smile. 'At least, I think so.'

Jocasta disagreed with his second assessment, but concurred with the first. Despite their easy conversation, when it had come to discussing the hatred of drugs which had motivated the elderly, fat-cigar smoking politician to construct the centre she had had a sneaking suspicion of something left unsaid.

She handed over a slip of paper from her folder. 'This is Mr LeBlanc's contact number.

He's available at the centre this afternoon, but then not for another couple of weeks.'

'So it'd be wise to see him today—before he changes his mind,' Christian remarked pithily, and lifted the telephone.

'Am I forgiven for arranging an interview without clearing it with you first?' Jocasta enquired, when a time had been fixed with the politician and a camera crew organised.

'You are.' He hesitated, as if wondering whether he should say more, but then looked at his watch. 'We're cutting it a bit fine, so I suggest we go and fill Barton in,' he said, and ushered her out of the office before him. 'How are you enjoying living in the French Quarter?' he asked, as they headed down the stairs.

Jocasta grinned. 'I like it. There's a great community spirit.'

'And you're pleased with the house that Max built?'

'Delighted. It's beautifully furnished and equipped down to the last teaspoon. It looks on to a private courtyard which has ivy-covered walls, trees and a fountain in the centre. It's beautiful, too.'

'But?' Christian said, when she suddenly frowned.

'Last night when I was drawing the curtains, there was a man in the courtyard. It was dark and difficult to see him clearly, but he seemed to be just standing there gazing at my window. When he realised I'd spotted him, he turned and hurried away back down the passage.'

'So you decided a potential axe murderer was lurking?'

When she had gone to bed Jocasta had thought about the man and the two strange telephone calls, and wondered if there might be a link. She had been beset by visions of someone breaking in, and the unease still lingered.

'Well——'

'Moving to a new neighbourhood, let alone a new country, jangles the nerves, but whoever it was would have had a perfectly innocent reason for being there,' Christian said, in firm reassurance. 'It could have been a visitor who was exploring the area.'

'Or someone who'd lost their way,' she said, deciding that, once again, she had been over-imaginative. 'I believe you're also in the process of moving to a new neighbourhood?'

'Two blocks away from you, set back off Royal Street. That's why I was enquiring about the French Quarter,' he told her. 'The property had been let go for a number of years, so I've been having it renovated. It's a stone two-storey house, with what used to be stables and slave quarters at the rear.'

Jocasta grinned, remembering her weekend walks. 'I've seen it. There are steps up to the front door and, on the first floor, french windows which open out on to a wide balcony with barley-sugar-twist wrought-iron railings?'

'That's the one.'

'It'll be lovely when it's finished.'

'Yes, but——' Christian grimaced '— I never realised how much would be involved in the renovation of an old building. The contractors have hit so many snags with the wiring, the plumbing—you name it—that it seems to be a case of lurching from one crisis to the next. I was due to relocate next month, then last week, but everything's way behind schedule and now I'm being pushed to vacate my apartment. The next date I've been given is in four weeks' time, but——' He shrugged. They had arrived at the presenters' room, where he reached past her to open the door. 'Is Barton around?' he asked Gaelene, who was leafing through a magazine.

The black girl shook her head. 'He's gone home. Said to tell you his throat's taken a turn for the worse and he needs to rest up, but he'll be recovered by tomorrow.'

Christian swung to Jocasta. 'Did you know about this?' he demanded.

'Did I know Barton wasn't here?' she asked, in bewilderment. 'How could I, when I've been in your office with you?'

'You were aware his throat was sore.'

'And?'

'He's unable to do the interview.'

Jocasta set her hands on her hips. 'Let me get this straight. I'm supposed to have let you fix everything with Mr LeBlanc in anticipation of Barton being out of action, and so now I step in? You'll be accusing me of plotting to overthrow the US government next!' Stalking to the nearest desk, she grabbed up the telephone and thrust it at him. 'Cancel the interview and rearrange it for later when Barton's around.'

'And risk LeBlanc opting out in the meantime?' Christian protested.

She flung an arm towards the black girl, who was watching their argument in bemused surprise. 'Gaelene can do it.'

After glancing at her colleague, he regarded her broodingly from beneath lowered brows. 'The interview is your baby so I guess you'd better stick with it,' he said, then added harshly, 'but I'm coming along, too.'

As the camera crew were arriving from one job and carrying on to another afterwards,

Christian drove her to the leisure centre in his Porsche. Sitting beside him as they sped out past the steel and glass towers of downtown New Orleans, Jocasta railed in fuming silence. Even though he had no experience of how she would get to grips with someone like the politician, his intrusion riled. It belittled. It was a transparent demonstration that he neither trusted her nor considered her capable. But she had shown him her notes and painstakingly detailed the slant she intended the interview to take, what more did he want? To dictate every question she asked? To command and countermand and interfere? She shot a resentful glance sideways. She did not need Big Brother watching over her.

On their arrival, she waited for Christian to don the jackboots and trample all over her. He didn't. To Jocasta's great surprise, he simply greeted the camera crew, introduced himself to Mr LeBlanc, then stood aside to put in some solid work as the polite bystander. Apparently she was to be left alone until she made what he considered a mistake, and *then* he would take charge and in so doing reduce her to pulp!

'We'll be filming the centre later, so I'll begin by asking you about the facilities which it provides,' she told the portly politician, when the lights had been set up in a white-walled, rust-carpeted office, 'and we'll take it from there. But if there's anything you don't feel comfortable with, please don't worry because it's absolutely no trouble for us to start again,' she said, in an overstatement which was designed to put him at his ease.

As the camera began to whirr Jocasta took a moment to get her brain into gear, then started on the questions. For someone who did not give interviews William LeBlanc spoke fluently and garrulously. As anticipated, he made a plea for donations, and everything rolled smoothly along until she asked him to explain what had inspired him to originally fund a centre. Then, although he continued to smile, again she felt he was not being entirely frank.

'I understand your horror at the damage drugs can do to young people, and your desire to give something back to the city which has done so much for you,' she said, after he had somewhat sentimentally described the debt he felt he owed to New Orleans, 'but you have spent a large amount of money. Your own money.'

William LeBlanc tugged at his floral waistcoat. 'I don't consider that a crime,' he said, a touch defensively.

'Neither do I. Your generosity is to be admired. However, it does make me wonder—must make anyone wonder—whether you had an additional reason for building the centre.'

'An additional reason?'

Jocasta pursed her lips. 'Maybe you have close personal experience of the drug problem?'

The suggestion had come off the top of her head, but now the politician's jowls shivered and tensed.

'You're figurin' ah consume chemical substances?' he demanded.

'No, but——' she acted on a hunch '—perhaps you have a child who does.'

'A child?' he echoed.

'A daughter or a son.'

William LeBlanc lurched up from his seat to wave a wildly flapping hand at the camera. 'Stop everything right there,' he barked, then furiously rounded on her. 'What is this—a blitzkrieg? I thought you were a well-bred young lady, but I was wrong. You're just another dirt digger, like the rest of your associates. Came acalling today in the hope of unearthing a scandal, did you——?'

'Hold on,' Jocasta protested.

'— I should have known!' Pulling a large white handkerchief from his pocket, he began agitatedly mopping his brow. 'You don't give a cuss about the value of what's being done here, all you're interested in is trapping me into making incriminating statements.'

Christian was standing to one side of the camera, and she cast him a quick glance. His brows were drawn tight together. He looked sombre. No doubt he was thinking that bird-brain had made a mess of things, as he had always known she would, she thought bitterly. Jocasta licked dry lips. But she was not beaten—not yet!

'If you do have a child who's on drugs, then talking about it in public would be both brave and helpful,' she told William LeBlanc quietly. 'So many people refuse to admit to addicts within their family because they believe it reflects badly on them, but anyone who has any sense knows it's a case of "there, but for the grace of God, go I."'

He gave her a guarded look. 'You think so?'

'I do,' she replied, her voice sincere and firm. 'I also think that if everyone was honest, barriers would be removed, assistance would come quicker, and the whole situation would be much easier. Don't you?'

Seconds, minutes, what seemed like hours, ticked by.

'Ah guess,' the politician said, and sucked in a breath. 'And you're right. Only thing you got wrong is the tense. Ah don't have a child who takes drugs, ah *did* have a child. That was my beloved son, William Junior, and he passed away five years ago when he was just nineteen. Ah built this centre in his memory,' he declared unsteadily, and pressed the handkerchief to his eyes.

Jocasta gazed at him in dismay. His shoulders were shuddering, his face contorted, and a moment later tears began to stream down his cheeks. Her heart went out to him. Poor old man, his son would have been the joy of his later years, the light of his life.

'I'm so sorry,' she said, and stopped, close to crying herself.

A reappraisal was required. She might have encouraged William LeBlanc this far and could probably encourage him further, but that would be unfair. She could not acquire what would undoubtedly be a choice interview—at his expense. Although the media had its piranhas who were happy to dive in at the deep end and bite into other people's tragedies, Jocasta did not number among them. Other people's feelings mattered, and she refused to land the politician with something he might later regret.

She looked at Christian again, and as his eyes met hers she knew he had recognised her de-

cision. Goodbye serious work, she thought
ruefully. Having botched this assignment he
would not give her a second chance. He
straightened and her stomach fluttered with
apprehension. He was going to haul her off into
a corner and lambast her for wasting his time,
wasting the camera crew's time, wasting an excellent TV opportunity. She waited. But instead, Christian quietly told the cameraman
and his colleague to leave and walked forward
to place a supportive arm around the sobbing
man's shoulders.

'If your son knew what you'd done he'd be
very proud,' he said.

'Ah—ah hope so,' William LeBlanc sniffed.

Jocasta gave a sympathetic smile. 'And his
death won't be in vain because you're saving
the lives of other young people.'

He blew his nose. 'Ah'm trying.'

'Please don't bother about the interview,' she
said. 'Either we can use just the first few
minutes or, if you prefer it, the whole thing can
be scrapped.' She looked defiantly at Christian.
'Yes?'

'Yes,' he agreed.

'And don't be alarmed about your secret
getting out. We won't say anything and neither
will the camera crew,' she assured him.

'Nobody will talk,' Christian promised, and he walked the politician over to the window where he spoke softly and comfortingly to him until he regained his composure.

'Ah figure maybe ah ought to come clean about my boy,' William LeBlanc reflected, as he stuffed his handkerchief back in his pocket. 'Ever since he first started on drugs ah've steered well clear of you media folks—thought somebody might have heard something and decide to ask a question and ah never dared risk it—but now ah think the truth should become public knowledge.' He smiled at Jocasta. 'It could help others, like you said.'

She frowned. If he wanted to speak of his own free will that was fine, yet there were bound to be repercussions.

'Maybe, but you must also consider the personal consequences,' she warned him seriously.

'Ah have, and you know something, young lady? Ah figure speaking out will also help me and my family. Mrs LeBlanc'd sure be relieved. She was never easy with the cover stories we made up and even now, so long after William Junior left us, she finds pretending a real strain.' He sat down on his chair again. 'Call in the camera guys and let's give it a go.'

'You're sure?' Christian demanded.

'Yup,' he declared, and the crew returned.

'I don't want to pry too far,' Jocasta told the politician, as she faced him again, 'so——'

'Ask me anything,' he insisted.

Filming resumed. At first her questions were tentative and the answers she received were stilted, but all of a sudden everything took off. In a spirit of true collaboration, William LeBlanc began to tell her about his son's tragedy. Nothing was hidden. It seemed as though the years of secrecy and subterfuge had been weighing him down, but at last he had the forum he needed to set the record straight. Was this why he had initially agreed to be interviewed? she wondered. Deep down, had he been yearning to speak?

'Is there a final message you'd like to give to other parents whose children have become hooked on drugs?' Jocasta enquired, as the interview wound to a close.

'To be open and above-board about the problem,' William LeBlanc declared.

'Thank you,' she said.

'Thank *you,*' he smiled.

Footage was taken of the centre and the teenagers involved in a range of activities, then the camera crew went off to their next assignment.

'Ah feel a heap better already,' the politician said, as Jocasta and Christian climbed back into the Porsche. 'You say the interview'll be shown this week?'

'Thursday,' Christian confirmed.

'Then ah must prepare myself to speak to a whole lot more of the media on Thursday,' he mused, sounding as though he could hardly wait.

Goodbyes were said, and they sped away. Now alert to the work which was waiting for him at the studios, Christian pushed his foot down hard.

'William LeBlanc might be ready to tell his tale again, but everyone will remember he gave his first interview—the crucial one—on *First Watch,*' he said, as he overtook every car on the freeway. Reaching out, he squeezed her knee. 'Thank you.'

When his hand remained on her knee, Jocasta sat very still. Christian was, she had realised, a tactile man. He would pat a back or, as had so recently happened, sling an arm around a shoulder in a sincere and easy gesture. His ability to touch was attractive, but she wished he were not touching *her.* She knew he had done so without thinking and because of the current euphoria, yet ever since she had suffered that rush of blood to the head and lowered her zip she had been disturbingly aware of him as a lean and virile male. But their relationship was difficult enough. The last thing she needed was an added complication in the form of an ever-present sexual dimension. The last thing she wanted was to feel the warm, intimate pressure of his fingers on her stockinged skin.

'As you appear to be making an attempt at the world land speed record, wouldn't it be safer to drive two-handed?' she enquired lightly, and he snatched his hand away as though her knee were red-hot. 'You told Mr LeBlanc that if he had second thoughts, the film could be withdrawn right up to the last moment,' Jocasta went on, needing to fill the silence which followed. 'So he could change his mind.'

Christian kept his eyes fixed on the road ahead. 'I don't think he will, though.'

'Neither do I,' she admitted. 'He spoke for ages; do you intend to cut some of it?'

'Not a thing. It's gripping stuff, and you made it happen.'

She shook her head. '*He* made it happen. I wasn't prepared to persuade him, so you were right— I'm not as tough as Barton.'

'Could be,' he agreed. 'However, I'm not so sure Barton would have asked LeBlanc if he had had an additional reason for building the centre.'

'It was an obvious question,' she protested.

'Yes, and yet when you're conducting an interview it's not always easy to spot the obvious. You did, and you thought fast on your feet.'

'So I'm not entirely a bimbo after all?' Jocasta enquired.

Christian gave her a quick look. 'That got right up your nose, didn't it? I apologise. I also want to apologise for accusing you of sharp practice where Barton and the interview were concerned.'

'Both apologies are accepted.' She hesitated. 'When Mr LeBlanc started to cry, I almost cried, too,' she confessed.

'I know. So?'

'I didn't keep cool and I wasn't professional.'

'Hell, Jocasta,' he protested, 'you're allowed to be unprofessional at an emotional moment like that.'

'Thanks. I prefer Jo,' she told him, thinking that this was the first time he had called her by her name.

'Hi, Jo.' He took his eyes off the road to smile at her. 'And I'm Chris.'

She grinned. 'Hello, Chris,' she said.

It seemed like a new and much better beginning.

# CHAPTER FOUR

THE next day's edition of *First Watch* went well, and for Jocasta *very* well. Whether her body clock had at last become attuned to her rising with the larks or if the boost provided by the LeBlanc interview was responsible, she did not know; but for the first time her sparkle came naturally. As ten o'clock drew near, satisfaction surged. Yesterday she had performed that necessary dose of television magic and won Christian over, and this morning her contribution to *First Watch* had been whole-hearted. The future looked rosy.

'Recently Jocasta went to visit an alligator, though it was not just any 'gator,' Gaelene told the viewers, 'and we're closing with what happened.' She wiggled her fingers. 'See y'all tomorrow.'

'Goodbye,' smiled Jocasta.

The camera moved to Barton, who had read the final news update and remained at the desk.

'Farewell, folks,' he said.

'Mr Gorgeous won't have any grumbles today,' Gaelene prophesied contentedly, as the

in-studio transmission ended and pictures of
the farmer and his toothy pet began to roll on
the screen.

Jocasta stood up and stretched. 'No way,'
she grinned.

'There'll be nothing,' said one of the girl as-
sistants, walking on to the set to collect the
glasses and jug of water from the table beside
the couch. 'A few minutes ago he received an
urgent phone call and he's had to leave. He
was pleased with the show, but there won't be
a post-mortem.'

Christian was sure to have noticed her zest
and would have made favourable comments—
comments to be savoured, Jocasta thought
wistfully—but never mind. She had played a
full and constructive part in carrying the show
along, and to know it herself was enough. As
she unfastened the microphone which had been
attached to the lapel of her pink linen blazer,
she kept haphazard track of the film, but suddenly her eyes switched to the clock on the
studio wall. Jocasta stared.

'The timing's out!' she yelped, in frantic
alarm. 'There are still three minutes and the
clip's almost through.'

Gaelene frowned. 'You sure?'

'Positive. *First Watch* is going to finish too
soon.'

Barton joined them. 'You must be mistaken,' he said soothingly. 'Chris would never get it wrong.'

'He has this time.' Jocasta pointed to the monitor where her final 'piece to camera' had begun. 'There are only thirty seconds until the end.'

'And Chris isn't here,' Gaelene said, tugging fretfully at one of her liquorice plaits. 'Gavin's in charge and—well, I hate to slam the guy but there have been occasions when he's loused up.' She began a tense countdown. 'Twenty... fifteen ... ten seconds.'

Barton squinted up to the windows of the control-room where technicians could be seen lolling in the after-show release and idly chatting. 'Holy cow! What do we do? You guys,' he shouted, waving his arms wildly around in an attempt to attract attention, 'Jo's film is almost through and there's——'

'Zero,' Gaelene announced in the fraught voice of doom, then gave a hoot of relieved laughter. 'False alarm!'

Jocasta stared at the screen. Instead of ending where it ought to have ended—with her suggestion that 'any lonely lady alligators out there might like to get in touch with Al'—the clip continued. As she smiled what she had believed to be her farewell smile, the camera

swung down to the alligator pawing her shoes,
swept up to reveal the fear written large across
her face, then panned backwards to show her
walking hurriedly away. Not much later, there
were shots of her dawning horror as the reptile
broke free, followed by a loving close-up of her
coming visibly unhinged. Jocasta saw herself
gallop off across the farmyard like someone
demented and make a desperate leap for safety.
Both gallop and leap were ungainly but it was
as she balanced precariously on her stomach
atop the wall that any last hope of dignity van-
ished. As her legs flailed, her skirt rode up and
there were flashes of pale thigh at the top of
her stockings, and—oh, no!—a glimpse of her
bikini briefs. When the celluloid Jocasta
eventually managed to straddle the wall and
disappeared from sight, the real one gave a
profound sigh of relief; but there was more
footage to come. Swinging to the barred gate
at the front of the pen, the camera zoomed in
again for a leisurely look and, to her chagrin,
she saw herself with face bright red and on all
fours, wallowing in the manure. Slowly and la-
boriously, a besplattered Jocasta rose up from
the mire like a monster rising up from the deep.
The camera lingered, and at the precise and or-
dained minute *First Watch*'s closing titles appeared on the screen.

'I wasn't aware Chip had continued to film. He never told me,' she said, turning furiously to Barton, 'but Christian had no right to use that out-take. OK, I explained how the alligator had——' Jocasta stopped dead. Her co-presenter had his hand over his mouth and his shoulders were going up and down. 'You're laughing,' she accused.

'Sorry,' he wheezed, 'but you were a real hoot.'

'A hoot?' she protested, then realised that, beside her, Gaelene was rocking back and forth, the victim of uncontrollable giggles.

'That's the most hilarious thing I've seen in ages,' the black girl gasped, wiping tears from her eyes. 'You'll have slayed 'em.'

'Slayed whom?' Jocasta demanded, then immediately it hit her that throughout the southern states a million and one couch potatoes would doubtless be convulsed with mirth, too. 'I expect I will,' she said tightly.

Barton gave her a closer look. 'You're not upset?' he enquired.

'Good grief, *no,*' she replied, and as laughter echoed from all around she managed a tinny burst of hilarity herself. 'It's just that, well, it's a bit of a surprise and I would have appreciated it if Christian had had a word with me first,' she said, and, with a grin nailed determinedly in place, she left the studio.

News of her antics seemed to spread like wildfire and there must have been repeat showings, for throughout the morning a veritable army of TKFM staff found their way to the presenters' room where she was attempting to work. Each wanted to say how they considered the alligator clip to be a classic—and insisted on reliving every last mortifying moment—but although Jocasta smiled and put on a brave face, inside she felt hurt and angry and deceived. The screening of the out-take was real kick-in-the-kidneys treatment. Christian's praise and apologies yesterday had lulled her into a false sense of security, she now realised. It had been her belief that his hostility had ended and he was content to have her working for him, but she had been woefully wrong. His secretary was asked to let her know immediately he returned, but when it reached early afternoon and he was still absent—and when the army kept coming—she left for home.

Her pea jacket and some other garments needed to be collected, so on reaching the French Quarter Jocasta walked to the dry cleaners. The woman before her had mislaid her ticket and there was a delay, and as she waited she gazed distractedly out of the window. She knew why Christian had shown the clip, she thought bitterly. A plan had been hatched between him and—— All of a sudden, Jocasta became aware of a man staring at her from a shop doorway across the street. A rough-looking character, he had shoulders the size of a well-exercised ox, a pock-marked complexion, and was wearing a blue anorak and scruffy corduroys. Had he recognised her as one of TKFM's presenters? Could be, and yet his stare seemed more intense and more intimate than those which usually came her way. He seemed to know her. Did she know him? she wondered. Yes, there was something about him which seemed familiar. She had seen him before, but where? Did he live around here or perhaps work at the studios? Jocasta was struggling to place him, when a grin stretched slowly across the man's face. It was a hot, lascivious and predatory grin. Hastily she lowered her gaze and kept it lowered, and a few minutes later when she risked another look the doorway was empty.

Plastic bags in both hands, Jocasta returned to the street. Afraid the grinner might be hovering, she cast a cautious look up and down but he was nowhere in sight. With a grateful sigh, she set off for home. She had walked one block and was turning a corner when, ahead

of her through the passers-by, she saw a tall
man with floppy brown hair and an athletic
stride. Her lips jammed together. Her blue eyes
went cold. It was Christian. A tan suede sports
coat thrown over his shirt and jeans, he was
going in the same direction. With explosive
steps Jocasta increased her speed, but as she
came within hailing distance he swung into a
delicatessen. A combination of anger and mo-
mentum kept her going, and she followed him
inside.

'Why, if it isn't the slimy, low-down, back-
stabbing rat,' Jocasta declared.

Christian wheeled round in surprise. 'Sorry?'

'So you damn well should be! I thought it
seemed odd that Debra was refusing all offers
of work, but now I understand,' she snapped,
her nostrils flaring, eyes blazing, psyche
smouldering.

He looked bewildered. 'Say again?'

'I realise there's a conspiracy.'

'What the hell are you talking about?' he
demanded.

'I'm talking about my alligator story which
appeared on *First Watch* this morning.' Jocasta
shone a frosty smile. 'You arranged for the
viewers to see the extended, unabridged
version, remember? Nothing would suit you
better than if, having been made to look a

clown, I decided to hit the door marked exit, would it?' she demanded, her voice soaring to a decibel level which had all the other customers turning to stare.

'Knock it off, will you?' he hissed.

'And if I walked out, just guess who'd walk straight back in—dull darling Debra!'

Christian's jaw tightened. 'Be quiet, *please*.'

'Even if you do have an allegiance to her there is such a thing as a code of honour,' Jocasta declared, furiously swinging the bags of dry cleaning and making him rear back, 'and what you've done does not——'

He turned to their alert-eared and rubbernecking audience. 'Isn't she fun?' he enquired. 'Stick around folks and Jocasta Chater will give you full details of what are——' he glared at her '—strictly in-company beefs. Then you'll be able to tell all your friends and they'll be able to tell all theirs and——'

She flushed and lowered her head. 'I'll shut up,' she muttered.

'And not before time. I'm buying myself a po-boy, would you like one? They're oversized sandwiches made from crusty French bread and they came into being during a 1920s streetcar strike,' Christian continued, in a chatty conversational tone. 'They can be stuffed with everything from soft-shell crabs to fried oysters to——'

'I know what po-boys are,' Jocasta said irritably.

She recognised the folly of so volubly losing her temper in public and was thankful that the other people in the shop seemed to have lost interest. But she wished it had not been him who had alerted her to her recklessness, and she objected to being treated like a child!

'Then do you want one? My favourite's shrimp and salad, topped with tomatoes, olives and egg wedges.'

Although Jocasta was in no mood to co-operate, the suggestion sounded mouth-watering—especially as, due to the nonstop stream of chuckling visitors, she had neglected to eat lunch.

'I'll have the same,' she told him stiffly.

'And a hot coffee to take out? I'm going back to my house,' Christian explained, 'so you can come with me and we'll talk. Coffee?' he repeated.

'Yes . . . thank you,' she made herself add.

When the scratch lunch had been bought, he took hold of her arm. 'Walk,' he instructed, and propelled her along the street to the grey stone house which she remembered.

'There was no need to frogmarch me!' Jocasta protested, shaking off his hand as they went inside. 'I told you I'd be quiet.'

'You could have had a relapse,' Christian said brusquely, and walked to the foot of a stripped pine staircase. 'I'm back,' he called up. 'Reached any decision yet?'

'Sorry, we're still working on it,' an invisible man informed him.

'Damn,' he muttered, and beckoned for Jocasta to follow him along the hall.

The floorboards were bare, the walls a brilliant white, and there was a strong smell of paint. Light and spacious, with interesting touches like a stained glass window halfway up the stairs and several arches in place of doors, the house *would* be lovely when the work was finished. He took her into an airy room which overlooked a rear patio, and which was obviously the living room. Walking over to the wide window-seats which edged a bay window, Christian put down the bag of sandwiches and coffee.

'You're wrong about a conspiracy,' he said, turning. 'The only reason Debra's refusing to work is——' his eyes hardened '—sheer bloody-mindedness, and if you did leave *First Watch* she wouldn't return.'

Jocasta regarded him coldly. 'No?'

'No. I'd veto it.'

'Oh.' She waited for him to say more, but he remained silent. She set down her plastic bags. 'So why deliberately rubbish me?' she demanded.

Christian looked hurt. 'I didn't.'

'You damn well did—you skunk, you jackal, you toad!' Jocasta burst out, blindly hurling any insult she could think of. 'When I told you about the alligator making chase I never imagined you'd go sneaking behind my back to check if Chip had it on film, nor that you'd then show it—again without saying a word. OK, you have editorial control, but I ought to have been consulted!'

'And if I'd asked, chances are you would have said no.'

'You can stake your life on it!'

'For pity's sake,' he said, his voice taking on an edge of impatience, 'it was great television.'

'Great?' Jocasta protested. 'It was ghastly!'

He shook his head. 'I knew the viewers would love it, and they did. I rang the studio an hour ago, and it appears that all morning the switchboard's been jammed with calls from——'

'From people falling about?' she broke in bitterly. 'And the viewers' enjoyment comes before any other consideration—like how I might feel? How very public-spirited!'

Christian frowned. 'I was under the impression you wanted to have a higher profile.'

'I didn't want to become a laughing stock!' she retorted, and, amid her fury, felt the unexpected sting of tears.

'Come on, it wasn't that big a deal.'

'It w-was,' Jocasta said chokily.

'And now you don't know whether to commit suicide or homicide?' he asked, and putting his arms around her he began to hypnotically stroke the nape of her neck. 'Honey, you're going over the top here,' he said gently.

His shoulder was broad and comforting and near, and she was besieged by the temptation to rest her head against it and weep.

'How could you make a fool of me like that?' she wailed. 'How could you humiliate me?'

Christian sighed. 'Jo, if I'd realised you were going to freak out like this I'd never have screened the bloody sequence.' He brushed a tendril of blonde hair from her brow. 'I know your career's of great importance and I'm sorry if——'

Jocasta pulled back to look at him. 'My career?' she queried.

'You're afraid the alligator clip will ruin things where your future as a high-purpose journalist is concerned.'

She frowned. Her work had not received a single thought; it was his *personal* betrayal which had caused the hurt, the inner bleeding, all her distress. But to realise she cared so much about his attitude towards her and to have been so devastated by what had seemed his treachery was both confusing and alarming.

'It won't help my credibility,' Jocasta declared and, aware that if she had cried on his shoulder she would have made a fool of herself for a second time, she stepped hastily from his embrace.

'It won't make any difference,' Christian refuted. 'Indeed, instead of appearing irritatingly perfect all the time, it's endearing to make a minor slip now and then.'

'A minor slip?'

'That's all this is,' he said firmly, 'and the viewers will love you for it—if they remember.'

'You think they won't?' Jocasta protested.

He sat down on the window seat, his long legs stretched out before him. 'Much as I hate to say this about the medium I love, the world does not revolve around television. It's more usually a matter of here today and gone

tomorrow, so by this time next week everyone'll have forgotten about your escapade.'

'Some hopes,' she muttered, shrugging off
the black greatcoat she wore over her pink suit
and sitting beside him.

He handed her a po-boy. 'OK, a few will remember,' he amended. 'But where's your sense
of humour? When you told me what had happened with Al you told it as a huge joke. Yes?'

'Yes,' Jocasta was forced to agree.

'I admit it did occur to me that when you
first     saw     the     out-take     you     could
be . . . disgruntled, but I reckoned you'd soon
come round.' Christian shone a smile. 'You are
coming round, aren't you?'

The curving of the Michelangelo lips would
have charmed birds out of trees, so how could
she resist?

'Slowly,' she conceded, and started to eat.

'The clip will have got you noticed,' he said,
when the sandwiches were finished and they
were drinking their coffee. 'And don't forget
that although the immediate response was
laughter, there'll also have been admiration at
your courage in standing there with the alligator and sympathy with your fright.'

'And lust at my wriggling backside,' Jocasta
added wryly. 'When I was in the dry cleaners
there was a man on the other side of the road

who had his eyes fixed on me,' she explained. 'A redneck, I think you'd call him. He appeared to know me, and to begin with I thought I must know him, too, but then he grinned.' She grimaced. 'It was a lecherous kind of grin.'

'You figure he'd been watching *First Watch*?'

She nodded. 'Yes.'

Christian's gaze flickered down her. 'While I don't deny that you possess an extremely nubile butt, you did only wriggle for a moment.'

'To me it seemed as if I was hung on that wall for ages,' Jocasta protested.

'If you'd blinked you'd have missed it,' he assured her.

'Well, at least now I'll be known for something other than being classy,' she remarked, as she drank the remainder of her coffee.

Christian laughed. 'You realise we're going to be inundated with requests for a repeat?' he said, mischief sparkling in his eyes.

'You wouldn't!'

'Not without your agreement,' he promised, then tilted his head. Someone was clattering down the stairs. 'Excuse me,' he said, and disappeared.

A long muffled conversation took place in the hall, but eventually the footsteps retreated and Christian returned.

'Another crisis has been surmounted,' he told her, with a broad grin of relief. 'The contractor had discovered some faulty brickwork around a doorway and he thought it was going to be serious. He called me about it at the studio this morning, which was why I had to leave. At one stage it seemed as though the entire wall might need to be knocked down and rebuilt, but after making extensive checks he now assures me the fault is relatively small-scale and can be easily remedied.'

'Phew!' she said.

'Quite.'

'I must go,' Jocasta said, and pulled on her coat. 'Thank you for the lunch.'

'You're welcome.'

'My performing slapstick this morning isn't going to fit in too well with being solemn and serious with Mr LeBlanc in a couple of days' time,' she commented, as they went along the hall. 'Not when you consider it'll be basically the same people who are watching.'

'It isn't a problem. I've rescheduled the LeBlanc interview for the evening news show,' Christian explained.

Her eyes opened wide. 'You have?'

'Not because of a clash, though I agree one's better avoided, but because the interview merits wider exposure than it'd get on *First Watch*. I

spoke to LeBlanc this morning and he's happy.
And so, I imagine, are you?'

'Delighted.' Jocasta gave him a teasing
glance. 'I didn't need to apply chloroform.'

'No, but——' Christian frowned and looked
away. 'Don't take your position at TKFM too
much for granted.'

Her fingernails dug deep into her palms.
Why must he ring a warning bell *now?* Why
did he have to spoil things? But the message
had been received and understood—despite the
LeBlanc coup she remained on trial. What was
it he did not trust? she wondered. Her capa-
bility as a television journalist or her moral
fibre? Did he still believe she had charmed Mr
Baumgarten into giving her a job? Jocasta
straightened. She resented his doubts, but she
refused to falter in her commitment.

'I won't,' she said lightly. 'This house must
have an interesting history,' she remarked, as
he opened the front door. 'I don't suppose
you'd agree to it being included in my French
Quarter series?'

Christian groaned. 'You never let up, do
you?'

'Forget about your house,' she said quickly,
'but surely a series might be worthwhile?'

'Do you work on the theory that even steel
bends under pressure?' he demanded.

Sensing some kind of victory, Jocasta grinned. 'I work on the theory that you don't give up on a problem until you're certain there's no way around it.'

'OK, submit your ideas for six clips of around five minutes each,' Christian said, and shook a finger. 'But remember, I'm making no promises.'

Jocasta smiled. 'I knew you'd see it my way.'

'Hey——' he started to protest, but she was already walking down the street.

# CHAPTER FIVE

'THE Formosan termite is a *big, big* issue which requires *major* exposure,' the residents' spokeswoman declared, speaking in tub-thumping italics. 'As I've explained, before you arrived we took a vote and it was the committee's unanimous decision that we require at least a full half-hour on air.'

'I'm sorry,' Jocasta replied, 'but, as I've explained——' for about the twentieth time, she thought wearily '—*First Watch* is a magazine-style programme and we're unable to devote so much time to just one subject. A ten-minute slot is the maximum.'

And if we spent half an hour on termites our viewers would be bored rigid, she added silently.

'But, hon, what we have here is a *nightmare situation,*' the woman insisted, and off she went again, spouting non-stop technical minutiae and arguing her case with gung-ho zeal.

As Jocasta was regaled with tales of infestation, extermination and pest-control test-sites, she sneaked a look at her watch. Because the committee had wanted to discuss their television debut at their regular evening meeting, her appointment had been fixed for eight o'clock, but now it had gone nine. She heaved a sigh. There was no doubt termites were causing severe damage and she felt sorry for the property owners, but after an hour of being bombarded all she wanted to do was go home.

'As *First Watch* is unable to provide the timespan you require, maybe we should scrub the idea,' she suggested, cutting purposefully into the spiel.

The woman's face dropped in comic and slack-jawed dismay. 'Scrub it?' she echoed.

Jocasta nodded. She knew she was taking a chance and that Christian would not be pleased if she returned empty-handed, but enough was enough. And from the start it had been obvious that the spokeswoman, an overweight brunette with aggressively plucked eyebrows, was positively drooling over the prospect of appearing on television.

'I could ask around at TKFM to see if anyone's interested in making a full scale programme,' she offered, her tone careless and non-hopeful, 'and if not, your committee might like to contact other stations.'

'Oh, no, no. It's fantastic that *First Watch* wants to feature our predicament and we sure appreciate the opportunity,' the brunette said, backtracking with haste. She pouted. 'And I guess half an hour would be kind of...hogging the limelight.'

'So we're agreed on ten minutes?' Jocasta enquired, becoming brisk and businesslike.

'Whatever you say, hon.'

Arrangements were made and not much later she departed. As Jocasta emerged into the night, she drew her overcoat closer around her. Because the woman lived in the French Quarter, albeit at an outer corner, she had walked to her house. It had been dark, but, although the area was off the tourist beat and quiet, home-going workers and other people had been around. Now the neighbourhood was deserted. Black clouds masked the moon, and, while street lamps shone circles of golden light, the stretches in between were shadowy and menacing. Warily, she eyed the bushes which grew in lush sub-tropical profusion around the houses and beside the pavement. Anyone could lurk behind them. Anyone who could pounce as she walked by. The townhouse was little more than a mile away, but maybe it would be wiser to take a taxi? Jocasta peered right and left. No taxis. Nothing. She set off walking.

The breeze rattled in the leaves of the palm trees, creating an eerie symphony. Something fast and furry—a cat? a rat?—darted out from a tangle of undergrowth and sped across in front, startling her. In the distance, a police siren wailed like a banshee. The atmosphere turned spooky. New Orleans could be a dangerous city, Jocasta thought, as she hurried along. Since her arrival there had been a murder almost every day. At the hum of a car behind her she spun hopefully round, but it was a private station wagon. Damn. About to continue, she hesitated. Beyond the vehicle and among a thicket of bushes, hadn't there been a furtive, fleeting movement? Her heart thudded against her ribs. Was someone there? Could that imagined attacker be lurking? Eyes narrowed, Jocasta searched the shadows then, as the breeze blew, gave a bleat of relief. The movement had been branches swaying.

She started to walk again, and when a couple of teenagers appeared beneath a distant streetlamp she felt happier. She was scolding herself for having been so foolish and so fearful when she noticed the rasp of footsteps behind her. She listened. Someone was following her. All of a sudden, the teenagers seemed very far away.

But if someone was walking in her wake, so what? her common sense demanded. It did not signify a threat. The person simply happened to be going somewhere, like her. They were not about to carry her off and rape her. She did not even know if the footsteps belonged to a man. Admittedly, they sounded heavy, but whoever it was could be a woman with a determined step. Should she look back over her shoulder and check? But if she did the person would think she was frightened, and she wasn't. Not really. As she turned a corner, Jocasta smiled. Not now, when the lights of the jazz clubs and restaurants were shining ahead.

A few hundred yards on and she was in a different world. Here couples strolled arm in arm, would-be diners discussed the attractions of glassed-in menus, traffic came and went. Yet, throughout it all, the rasping footsteps continued. Able to be brave, Jocasta cast a quick look back. Her brow puckered. It was difficult to be certain, but at the same moment as she had turned her head hadn't someone plunged out of sight into a doorway? Whether or not, there were several people on the pavement behind her and identifying one as the follower was impossible.

She kept on walking, kept her ears peeled. At first, street noise blocked out the distinctive sound, but then there was a lull and the footsteps came again. Jocasta crossed the road, turned a corner and, in time, another. Off and on, some way behind, the footsteps continued. A chill shivered through her bones. Was the person going exactly her way by accident or could she be being stalked? If so, there were people around, she comforted herself, and she had almost reached home. All it needed was for her to walk one more block, go down the passageway and—Jocasta's heart missed a beat. The passage was not long, but it was dark; and the courtyard was gloomy, too. Still, she had a good start, and if she hurried would be indoors and safe within minutes.

Stealthily she increased her walk to a jog and, although she strained to listen, heard no accompanying, accelerating rasp. Whoever the determined tread had belonged to, they were no longer behind her. She had lost them. Thank you. Thank you. Jocasta was lolloping contentedly into the passage, when, all of a sudden, footsteps sounded again and a male voice shouted a restraining, 'Hey!' She tensed like a coiled spring. Fear rose up in her throat. She *was* being stalked and, although she had not heard him, her pursuer must have put on speed too, for he was closer than she would ever have imagined. Much closer.

Jocasta bounded forward, but a split second later the clatter of feet on stone warned that he, too, had entered the passage. At full tilt, she ran. And heard him hot on her heels. She was exhorting herself to run faster, faster, when her foot suddenly slithered on the uneven cobblestones. Jocasta skidded, stumbled and would have fallen headlong if a hand had not reached out to grab her arm and keep her upright.

'Get—get away from me!' she panted, batting blindly at the hand in an effort to free herself. 'Leave me alone!'

'I only wanted to talk to you,' her captor protested.

Her head jerked round. 'Christian!' she gasped.

'Ten out of ten for recognition,' he said drily.

It took her a minute to catch her breath. 'I—I thought someone was chasing me. You see, I heard——' Jocasta froze. Over his shoulder, a bulky male figure had loomed at the street end of the passage and, with a hand shading his eyes, was peering in. It must be the man who had been following her! 'Put your arms around me,' she hissed.

Christian looked bemused. 'Sorry?'

'And kiss me.' Grabbing hold of his tie, she yanked him towards her. 'Quick!'

'What——?'

'*Please,*' Jocasta begged, and when he hesitated she pressed her lips to his.

Maybe the urgency of her appeal had penetrated or he might have been stunned by surprise, whichever Christian made no further objection. To begin with, the kiss was a chaste, neutral affair, but gradually it changed. Jocasta let go of his tie and without thinking what she was doing—just doing what came naturally—wound her arms around his neck. He pushed two hands into her unfastened coat and spread them on her waist. Together they stood, body to body, mouth against mouth. The heat which radiated from his lips was seductive and sent a quicksilver surge of desire chasing through her. As though in response, he drew her closer and, easing back his head, Christian brushed his mouth across hers. Soft and sensual, his lips moved until it seemed as though every nerve-end in her body was awakened and clamouring, wanting more. Restlessly, she stirred and he pulled her into him, then, with an incoherent murmur, he opened his mouth on hers and started kissing her with a deep and demanding hunger.

Jocasta's heart turned over. Her fingers curled tight into the thick dark hair at the nape of his neck. All sense of time and place disappeared. Her only awareness was of the strong arms around her, the scent of his skin, the moist delights of his mouth. When she had been kissed before, it had never been like this. It had never felt so exciting, so overwhelming, never possessed such *sizzle*. This was what 'sexual chemistry' meant, she thought dimly.

Suddenly, Christian drew back. 'That's right,' he said, breathing heavily. 'Wait until my defences are down and then take advantage of me.'

Jocasta looked at him in dazed wonderment. 'What—what do you mean?'

'I mean you kissing me,' he said, and his voice gathered an edge. 'One minute you're ripping off your clothes and the next you're——'

'I didn't rip off any clothes and I didn't kiss you. Not properly,' she protested. 'You kissed me.'

'Like hell.'

She bristled. 'You did!'

'You made the first move—and almost throttled me in the process,' Christian retorted, rubbing savagely at his neck.

'I wish I had!' Jocasta declared, bewildered to discover that after being locked so passionately in his embrace, she was now under attack. 'There was only one reason why I asked you to kiss me,' she informed him tartly, 'and that was because I thought it would act as a deterrent.'

'Deterrent against what?'

Belatedly, she looked to the end of the passage. It was empty. 'I was walking back from the termite woman's house when I heard footsteps,' she started to explain. 'Someone seemed to be following me, so when I neared home I put on a spurt. I was convinced I'd shaken them off until I heard the sound of footsteps again, and a shout.'

'Me,' Christian said.

'You.'

His mouth twitched. 'At which point you took off like a crazed rabbit.'

'I panicked,' Jocasta agreed stiffly. 'But a second or two after you'd caught me, a man peered into the passage. I realised he could be a fan, and I thought that if he thought I had a boyfriend it might cool his ardour. So—so I suggested a kiss.'

'How long had the guy been following you?' Christian demanded.

She scrunched up her brows. Had that movement she had glimpsed in the bushes really been the breeze? 'It could have been all the way,' she said.

'What did he look like?'

'Er...thick-set.'

'That's it?'

Jocasta nodded. 'I did turn round to see who it was, but he hid in a doorway—at least, I think he did.'

'So the only time you saw him was just now? But you were so intent on dragging me into a clinch, you didn't get much of a look?'

'That is correct,' she said primly.

'How do you know the guy who peered in was the guy who'd been following you?' Christian asked. 'The way the pair of us sprinted in here would have made anyone curious.'

Jocasta frowned. 'I don't know,' she admitted.

'You said someone "seemed" to be following and you "think" they hid in a doorway, but the reality is that it's all supposition.'

'Well...yes, and yet the footsteps did stick with me the whole way, despite me crossing streets and turning corners,' she defended.

'Which could have been pure chance.'

'I did wonder about that myself,' she had to concede.

Christian flung her an exasperated look. 'Someone misdials and you interpret it as a nuisance call. A guy stood in your courtyard is marked down as acting suspiciously. And now a citizen out for an evening stroll is full of evil intent? You sure have a taste for transforming ordinary events into the dramatic.'

'People who appear on television *are* followed,' Jocasta protested. 'All it needs is for a fan to take one look, become besotted, and they start stalking them. And sometimes they stalk them everywhere, morning, noon and night.'

'OK, harassment can be an occupational hazard,' he said impatiently. 'But you're not being harassed, you're just becoming paranoid! There's not a single shred of evidence to show you've been followed. All you can come up with is some airy-fairy——'

'You wanted to talk to me,' she reminded him, in a tart change of subject.

Because she could not prove someone had been following her, it did not mean they hadn't. It was true that she was not certain they had, either—and yet the feeling of having been under threat persisted.

Christian nodded. 'About the LeBlanc interview.'

'Did something go wrong?' Jocasta asked, suddenly anxious because the film had been due to be shown that evening.

'Everything went beautifully,' he assured her. 'I'd called to check on progress at my house——' he grinned '—there's plenty—and as I was driving back I saw you. It struck me that instead of waiting until morning I could have a word now, so I stopped the car and——'

She interrupted him. 'When you got out you didn't notice anyone who might have been following me?'

Christian gave an irritated sigh. 'No. I'm parked outside a café a hundred yards away,' he continued, and gestured towards the street, 'so why don't we grab a cup of coffee and talk there?'

Jocasta hesitated. After first insisting she was responsible for the kissing and then calling her paranoid, a curt, 'No, thanks, it's too late,' was what he deserved. But. A coffee would go down well and, besides, she was eager to hear what he had to say.

'Lead on,' she said.

A comfortable place of dark polished wood, maroon velvet upholstery and with etched glass dividers between the tables, the café's old-fashioned appearance came accompanied by efficiently modern service. A smiling waitress swiftly introduced herself, seated them and served steaming cups of good French coffee.

'Y'all sure you wouldn't like something more?' she coaxed. 'We do a real nice line in filled croissants, quiches and homemade desserts. Folks come from miles around for a taste of our pecan pie.'

'Fancy a piece?' Christian enquired, when Jocasta looked interested.

She nodded. 'Please.'

'Two,' he said, grinning at the woman who was noticeably charmed. 'As I was leaving the studios this evening William LeBlanc rang,' he explained. 'He wanted to thank you for suggesting he should talk about his son and to say it's the best thing he could have done. Apparently the interview had barely gone off the air before his phone was busy with every political bigwig in the south wanting to shower him with admiration and praise. But what matters most is that both he and his wife feel you've turned their lives around. It seems Mrs LeBlanc had been suffering from depression, but already she's taken on a new lease of life and LeBlanc's also been revitalised—which he reckons is all due to your understanding.'

'That's great,' Jocasta said happily, 'but you were understanding too, so you had a hand in it.'

'Only a small one,' Christian protested, and, between eating mouthfuls of pecan pie, he started to reminisce about the circumstances of the interview.

As they chatted, Jocasta found herself looking at his hands—the hands which had squeezed her knee, and brushed the hair from her brow, and so recently held her waist. He had long strong fingers with square blunt cut nails, and there was a smattering of fine golden-brown hair on his wrists which, when he gesticulated, glinted in the subdued light. Christian frequently gesticulated, and he often ran a hand through his hair, she remembered—in a way which made you want to join in. He had other appealing habits, like the loosening of his tie which made him seem oddly little-boy-lost and vulnerable. And the tossing of his jacket over one shoulder. And——

'Did you organise the termite story?' he enquired.

Jocasta blinked. 'The termites? Oh, yes. Though the committee are going to be disappointed,' she said, and galloped off into a recital of their main feature expectations and her subsequent trimming.

The dessert finished, the waitress reappeared to receive their compliments and to replenish their cups.

'About Debra,' Christian said, when they were alone again.

'What about her?' Jocasta demanded. His voice was serious and his expression grave—

and she was immediately thrust on to the defensive. 'If you're about to say that, as with the LeBlancs, I turned her life around—except the wrong way—then——'

'Jo, the person responsible for Debra's flight, hysteria, becoming a recluse et cetera is me,' he said heavily.

'You?' she protested.

'Max Baumgarten may have given her the push, but I was the one who made it happen.' Christian took a mouthful of coffee. 'It's time I put the record straight, and that means explaining about my relationship with Debra. It also means starting at the beginning——' he gave a strained smile '—which ain't easy.' Folding his arms, he rested his elbows on the table. 'I told you I'd worked in France, but what I failed to say was that I was there because I was married to a French girl.'

Unwilling to betray Barton's confidences, Jocasta gave a non-committal nod.

'However, two years ago she was killed when a car she was in crashed outside Paris,' he said, the tautness of his voice making it plain that his wife's death remained a difficult subject. 'My immediate reaction was a virulent hatred of France, and within days of the funeral I'd packed in my job and come back to the States.

TKFM were looking for a news director, so I walked straight in.'

'Lucky,' she remarked.

'Very. Talking about Martine was too painful at that stage, so I avoided it by letting everyone at the studios assume I was single and always had been.' He frowned. 'Which, unnecessarily, they still do. In those early days, so long as I was working I was fine,' Christian continued, 'but the minute I went home I fell apart.'

'You'd put your life into compartments,' Jocasta observed.

His eyes met hers. 'You've done it, too?'

'Once. It was the only way I could function.'

'And with me,' he said, and they shared a smile of understanding. 'On my return my parents had suggested I move in with them,' he carried on, 'but, apart from being a big boy now, I desperately needed time on my own to work things through, and so I leased an apartment. However, working anything through seemed to be beyond me, and in between bouts of staring angrily at the wall I started to drink. Never enough for it to affect my work, but far too much. This went on for about a year, then one day I had the granddaddy of a hangover which was impossible to conceal and Debra was sympathetic. By this time my folks had grown weary of my feeling sorry for myself as the tortured widower and were suggesting I brace up, so her sympathy was most acceptable. Little things make big differences,' he said laconically. 'Until that point I'd never noticed Debra on a man-to-woman basis. She was simply a presenter on one of my programmes—though I'd begun to toy with the idea of removing her,' he added.

'You wanted rid of her?' Jocasta said, in surprise.

'She was centre highway, remember? However, because I was looking for a shoulder to cry one, I guess, I invited her out to dinner.' Christian lifted his spoon and began making aimless patterns in the sugar. 'Debra was so full of concern and so willing to listen that I confessed I'd been married and that my wife had died, and I told her about Martine.' He frowned. 'Just general things. I'd regarded the dinner as a one-off, but a couple of weeks later Debra asked me out and I accepted. You see, after talking to her I'd started to feel livelier and had cut down on the hooch. Now I'm sure it was coincidence— I had to emerge from my trough of despair some time—but then it seemed as though Debra was instrumental.'

'And you were grateful?'

'Deeply, with the result that the dinners became a regular occurence—though I asked her to keep quiet about them.'

'Why?'

'I didn't want other people to get the wrong idea and start thinking of us as a couple, because we weren't. We were simply friends. However, one night she suggested we go to bed together.'

'*She* suggested?' Jocasta enquired.

'Debra was heavily into equality,' he said, in a dry voice.

'And out of gratitude you agreed, though you weren't attracted to her?' she asked protestingly.

Christian expelled a long breath. 'Gratitude played a part, plus Debra was so undemanding that being in her company was kind of a balm. But also I hadn't slept with a woman since Martine's death and, like any other red-blooded male, I have needs. I know it sounds lousy and I'm not proud of myself, but in a weak moment——' He spread his hands. 'However, the next time Debra broached the subject, I made it plain I wasn't interested in an involvement and said thanks, but no, thanks. Her response was that she realised I was still emotionally wound up in my wife, but where was the harm in a romp now and then? So, we . . . romped.'

'You lived together?' Jocasta asked.

'Hell, no! Our affair was casual and spasmodic. I didn't spend one whole night with her—ever.'

'Why not?'

'Because I never wanted to, but also because I was determined to keep a distance between us.' Christian gouged a crater in the sugar bowl. 'I assumed that because our relationship was static for me, it was the same for Debra—but I was mistaken. I didn't notice it at the time, but looking back it's obvious that over the months she started to regard me as her property, and—well, generally became more intense.' He sighed again. 'Everything was blasted out into the open the day I told her I was arranging to buy the house. Debra was eager to take a look, so we went round and before I knew it she was saying why didn't "we" paint this room that colour, and were "we" going to use this one as a study, and why didn't "we" have a conservatory?' He filled in the crater and sat back. 'I'd bought the place because I wanted somewhere of my own and because property is a good investment, but she took it to be a declaration of impending marriage!'

Jocasta suppressed a smile at his indignation. 'Oh, dear.'

'When I explained that I intended to live there alone, there were howls of outrage. She accused me of stringing her along, but that was pure fabrication. I'd always been up-front about our affair's having no emotional content. I'd never told her I loved her. I'd never once mentioned our having a future, dammit.' Christian glowered. 'However, Debra insisted it had been "understood" and, after claiming to be an ardent feminist, now declared she wanted the traditional things which every woman wants—a husband and kids!'

'You make it sound like a sin,' Jocasta demurred.

'She made me feel as if *I'd* sinned,' he thrust back. 'She went on and on about how her biological clock was ticking and how I'd made her waste valuable time. And how I'd used her. Then she jumped lanes and said that if we lived together I'd learn to love her, and could we give it a go? From being undemanding, she'd become ultra demanding. Naturally, I dismissed the idea outright but she insisted it was an option.' Christian pushed the hair back from his brow with impatient fingers. 'After that, the sensible thing would have been to make a clean break, but she made me feel so guilty. I mean, I *had* used her—for sex and as a crutch to help me through the trauma of Martine's death.'

'You didn't continue your affair?' she protested.

'No way! But a few days later, when Debra asked me to go to her place to talk things over, I agreed. Only she didn't want to talk once, she wanted to talk week after week after week.'

'In the hope that you'd change your mind?'

He nodded. 'And because I was dumb enough to continue seeing her because I wanted to be kind, she kept on hoping. Yet every time it was the same old arguments, the same protests, the same appeals, again and again.'

'This is why Debra was distracted?' Jocasta enquired.

'Yes. I know I told you she wasn't, but that was after she'd filled my answering machine with accusations, yet again, and I was feeling all knotted up.' Christian drank some more coffee. 'Over the months, Debra's behaviour on screen deteriorated. She gave the minimum. For a while I closed my eyes to it, but eventually I spoke to her—and she coolly informed me that, yes, she knew her performances were flat but it was my fault, and if I wanted it to stop I knew what to do. The bloody woman was damaging her own reputation and that of *First Watch,* and holding me to ransom!'

Jocasta frowned. 'But if she was so upset, she might not have been able to help her attitude.'

'She could have tried,' he protested, 'but she didn't. Instead Debra *flaunted* her lack of interest.'

'And hell hath no fury like . . .' she mused.

Christian nodded. 'Revenge was the root cause. Things reached such a state that eventually I bit the bullet and told Max she had to go—though I felt a real low-down, back-stabbing rat,' he added, drily quoting her own words at her. 'Because people had remarked on her poor showing to him, he was in full agreement, and we left it at that. Staff changes had always been my responsibility, so I started to look around for an alternative presenter and, gently, gently, began extolling the merits of the women's afternoon programme to Debra. There was soon to be an opening there,' he explained.

'You think she'd have switched?' Jocasta asked.

'Surprisingly, yes. She finally seemed to be realising the two of us were finished and that her behaviour could only be self-destructive. I was psyching myself up to suggest the change when Max bowled back in from his business trip.'

'And announced the imminent arrival of a *wunderkind?*' she said, being pertly flip because he had frowned.

'Right. At that precise moment, you were a complication I could have well done without,' he remarked pungently.

'You said you'd veto Debra's return. Couldn't you have vetoed me?'

'I thought about it, but Max was so damned *keen*. Also we were in immediate need of a third presenter because, without consulting me, he'd informed Debra that her days on *First Watch* were numbered and she'd already rushed off—in high dudgeon, as they say.'

'She blamed you?'

'In total.'

Jocasta frowned. 'You didn't explain how Mr Baumgarten had forced things?'

'I didn't and I haven't. What's the point when, basically, her being ousted was because of me?'

'Do you think her refusal to work and see people might be yet more revenge?' she queried.

He nodded. 'The things she's said on my answering machine have made it clear the aim is to make me suffer, and, believe me, I *have* suffered.'

'Does she ring often?' Jocasta asked.

'For a long time she called every day to spell out in detail how I'd ruined her life, but——' Christian gave a small smile '—that last mammoth denunciation seems to have been the turning point, because I haven't heard anything from her since. And I *have* heard a rumour about her negotiating with a Texan network.'

'Sounds like she's recovering.'

'Touch wood.'

Jocasta looked at her watch. 'Time I was tucked up in bed,' she decided.

'You'll need someone to deflect all those guys waiting to come at you with their machine guns, so I guess I'd better walk you home,' he said, with mock weariness.

'Thank you, Sir Galahad,' she replied pertly, and made him laugh.

'It's Mardi Gras in a couple of weeks,' Christian remarked, as they crossed the courtyard. 'How would you like to go out on the streets to report on the parades and do some interviewing?'

She frowned. 'I understood that the evening news presenters covered Mardi Gras?'

'They do, but I'm adding you to the team— temporarily. You'll need to do a crash course on the history, though I doubt it'll be a problem.'

Jocasta gave a wide smile. 'None,' she assured him.

'The carnival dominates our coverage to the tune of around twelve hours a day,' he explained, as they reached the townhouse. 'The big parades hit the streets a week or so before, though you'll be reporting on Mardi Gras itself. The programmes attract a wide local audience and networks from all over the States also use our footage, so——' Christian broke off to listen. 'Your phone's ringing.'

Jabbing her key in the lock, Jocasta opened the door, flicked on the living-room light and dashed across to the bureau. 'Hello?' she said, as she lifted the receiver.

There was a sinister male chuckle and then someone started to speak.

## CHAPTER SIX

CHRISTIAN saw the colour drain from her face.

'Something wrong?' he asked.

Placing her hand over the mouthpiece, Jocasta nodded. 'I know everyone needs a hobby,' she said, with a shaky attempt at humour, 'but there's a man on the line who apparently gets his kicks from telling women what he'd like to do to them—in graphic detail.'

He came forward and took the telephone from her. For a moment or two he listened, his face hardening. 'The guy's sick,' Christian denounced, in disgust.

'A weirdo,' she agreed, but when he went to angrily replace the receiver, she stopped him. 'I know slamming down the phone is the obvious reaction,' Jocasta said, remembering how the other day when she had—maybe—received the nuisance call, she had told the caller to get lost, 'but the experts' recommendation is that you *don't* react. What you should do is put the telephone on its side and stay out of earshot until the talk peters out. That way, the caller's denied the excitement of the shock or horror which he wants.'

'Makes sense,' Christian agreed, and lifted a cushion from the sofa. 'But let's put this over the damn phone while we're waiting. I was telling you how other networks take the choicest parts of our Mardi Gras footage,' he carried on. 'It means that if you should tape an especially interesting interview it could be shown nationwide. And that could mean fame.'

Jocasta frowned at the muffled receiver. 'Fame?' she said, wondering if the man was still spewing his vile language, wondering why he should have dialled her particular number on this particular evening, wondering whether there could be any connection with her being followed? *If* she had been followed.

'Appear on a major network and one of their executives could spot you. They're always on the lookout for anyone with the potential to be a star, because stars are a key weapon in the battle for viewers. So——' Christian took hold of her shoulders and turned her around to face him. 'You're not listening to a word I'm saying.'

She flashed a smile. 'Sorry.'

'Unfortunate though it is, obscene phone calls are a fact of modern life,' he pointed out gently.

'I know,' Jocasta said, looking up at him with wide blue eyes. 'Eight million a year are reckoned to be made in the UK. Amazing I've never received one before, isn't it?' she said unsteadily.

His hands tightened on her shoulders. 'Jo, I know it's distressing, but it's a long way from fatal.'

He was right. The call was unpleasant, period. And in imagining a link she had been allowing her thoughts to run riot. She took a breath. Her imagination must be kept under control. She would not be accused of paranoia again.

Jocasta nodded brightly, and tossed a glance over her shoulder. 'Will you check whether buddy-boy's vocal chords have seized up yet or shall I?'

'I'll do it.' Christian lifted the cushion, listened for a moment and then grinned. 'All clear. Suppose we have a drink?' he suggested, when the phone had been replaced.

She gave what was intended to be a casual laugh. 'To steady my nerves?'

'It's mine I'm worried about,' he said, and grimaced. 'Calls like that may be common-place, but it's the first time I've listened in on one. I believe they're described as verbal and mental rape and it's certainly left me feeling...dirty.'

'So you'd like a stiff brandy followed by a scrub-down in a hot bath?' Jocasta enquired, her tone determinedly light. 'The bath's no problem, but I'm afraid the brandy is. I've yet to buy any alcohol and all I can offer is fruit juice, cola, tea or coffee.'

'Another cup of coffee would go down fine.' She took off her coat. 'Give me two minutes.'

'You said you'd once needed to compartmentalise your life,' Christian remarked, as she handed him a mug and sat, legs tucked beneath her, at the other end of the sofa.

'Now you're attempting to divert my thoughts.' She grinned.

'It's that ham-fisted? Even so, I'm interested to know what happened.'

'Well, a couple of years ago I fell in love with a man who, as time passed, began to resent my career.' Jocasta took a sip of coffee. 'Oliver was in banking and worked normal hours, whereas my job as a reporter for a nightly news programme tied me up most evenings and meant I never knew where I'd be at any given time during the day. A story broke, I was dispatched and——' She shrugged. 'You know the score. I broke endless arrangements and rushed in late on so many occasions that Oliver got madder and madder. He accused me of being obsessed with my work.'

'Maybe if he'd been in television too, he'd have been more understanding,' Christian suggested.

'Maybe, though he was right— I was obsessed. My career came a definite first in those days.' She sighed. 'Anyway, Oliver finally lost patience and said I must choose between him and the job.'

'This was a serious relationship? The kind which ends in marriage?' he enquired.

'Yes.'

'But you chose the job?'

'I did, though it was a decision I quickly regretted. It broke my heart when we parted and the year which followed was the worst in my life,' she said, and sighed again, remembering. 'But by putting everything into mental boxes I managed to be all cheerful efficiency at work and restrict my weeping to when I was alone.'

'You were still in love with him?'

'For a long time.'

'And now?'

'It's over. But now I have my priorities straight and I know that my personal life is more important than my career. Much more.' Jocasta gave a wistful smile. 'Oliver was another reason for my coming to the States. Maybe *the* reason.'

'How so?'

'We lived in the same neighbourhood and shared many of the same friends, which made it impossible to avoid both seeing him and hearing about him. The proximity had been agony during that first year, but even when the emotional thing faded I was still being constantly reminded of my selfishness and it wore me down. I was wishing I could get away, at least for a while, when Mr Baumgarten—— Oh, no!' she exclaimed, as the telephone suddenly rang.

Christian scowled. 'Guess who.' Striding to the bureau, he lifted the receiver, listened, and, in a fury of violently well-picked epithets, proceeded to tell the caller exactly what he thought of him and his nauseating habit.

'That might not be the recommended procedure,' Jocasta remarked wryly, as the telephone clattered down, 'but I doubt he'll be calling again.'

'I wouldn't be too sure,' he said, with a frown. 'The fact that he rang back now means he's taken a note of the number.'

'I'll leave the phone off the hook tonight,' she decided.

'Do that,' Christian said, and finished his coffee. 'I must go. The guy didn't give any hint that he might be aware of your identity?' he enquired, as she opened the front door.

Abruptly agitated, Jocasta looked at him. 'No. Did he say anything to you?'

'Nothing.'

'Thank goodness!'

'There's no need to be frightened,' Christian said, when her eyes flickered beyond him and out into the darkness.'

'I'm not.'

'Liar.'

Jocasta gave a shame-faced smile. 'The call was a bit unsettling.'

'It was a lot unsettling.' He studied her. 'Are you going to lie awake all night worrying about it?'

She straightened her shoulders. 'I don't think so.'

'I do,' he said. 'I also think that tomorrow you're going to be sleepwalking your way through *First Watch*.' Christian pushed his hands into his trouser pockets and stared at the ground for a long moment, then he raised his head. 'Suppose I stay until dawn?'

'Sleep here?' Jocasta said, in surprise.

He nodded. 'It'd give you a peaceful night, and mean you'd be bright-eyed and bushy-tailed in the morning.'

'Yes, but——'

'If you're worried about people gossiping, who's going to know?' he demanded, a touch impatiently.

'No one,' she admitted.

'And you'd prefer not to be alone? Honest answer,' Christian insisted.

'Yes.'

He gestured towards the off-white, over-stuffed sofa. 'I'll use that.'

'No need,' she said, bemused by the speed of his decision-making. 'There are two bedrooms.'

The coffee-mugs were cleared away, the house secured, and Jocasta led the way upstairs.

'There's a new toothbrush in the bathroom cabinet,' she said, and grinned back over her shoulder, 'but I'm fresh out of man-sized pyjamas.'

'Never wear them,' he replied.

Her mood had been light, but all of a sudden she was stricken by images of Christian sleeping naked and smooth-skinned in the room next to hers. They were disturbing images and yet foolish ones—for his statement and manner were resolutely matter-of-fact. That they were to spend the night alone together did not appear to bother him one bit. Any awareness of a sexual dimension was in her mind only.

'Um...if you'd like to use the bathroom, I'll prepare your bed,' Jocasta gabbled, and, with hasty directions as to what was where, she retreated in search of sheets.

The bed made up, she went to her room. Splashing sounds had indicated that her visitor was taking a shower and, as she undressed, she decided to wait until his bedroom light had been doused before she emerged. That way they would avoid further contact—which had become important. Her pale blue silk night-dress was pulled on and covered with a matching robe. Jocasta was brushing her hair when the splashing ceased, and not much later footsteps padded and a click of a switch indicated that Christian had settled down for the night. Going hotfoot into the bathroom, she creamed her face, cleaned her teeth, and had a quick shower. She was making her return along the darkened landing when a tall figure suddenly appeared from the doorway of the spare room. Startled, she gazed at him. Bare-chested and barefoot, all Christian wore was a pair of brief navy underpants, presumably pulled on for decency's sake.

'You weren't thinking that the foulmouth on the phone might be the same guy who followed you?' he demanded.

'It—it did occur to me,' she faltered.

Without his clothes Christian seemed much bigger and more...rawly masculine, she thought, unable to tear her eyes away. Not exactly a closet Rambo, but aggressively male. His shoulders and arms were well-muscled and his chest was hairy—the dark curls forming a thick covering over his pectorals and then marching in a vertical line across his stomach and down. His thighs were also muscular and had a lighter covering of hair.

'But when he looked into the passage he saw the two of us and the guy's hardly likely to call if he knew you had a man around,' he said.

'Yes. Er— I mean, no.'

Jocasta's cheeks burned. She was not sure what she meant. All she could focus on was the hair which flopped appealingly over his brow, the width of his shoulders, the gleam of his skin in the muted light. Accepting his offer to stay had been a mistake, she thought despairingly. She would not lie awake fretting over the man on the phone; she would be tossing and turning, unable to sleep because Christian was in the next room.

'So the call happened by chance,' he concluded.

'I— I expect it did,' she got out chokily.

Christian frowned. 'Well, goodnight.'

'Goodnight.'

Both should have turned, yet neither of them moved. Instead, still and silent, they gazed at each other through the shadows. The oxygen seemed to seep from the air and Jocasta found it difficult to breathe.

'We need our sleep,' Christian said, sounding as though he was arguing a point in an internal debate.

'Yes.'

Again no one moved.

'Hell, *Jo*!' he complained, and there was a throb in his voice. 'I knew you meant trouble the first time I saw you. Not just at work, but——'

'But what?' she asked, when he stopped.

'But like this,' he said, and reached out his arms.

His mouth was hot on hers, his tongue a drugging invader. Her eyes shut and held close against his chest, Jocasta felt the beating of his heart—or was it hers? Christian ran his hands down the curve of her spine, pressing her against him and forcing an awareness of the hard muscles of his thighs. A giddy heat suffused her and beneath the thin silk her breasts lifted and tautened, their rose-red nipples becoming erect.

'When I kissed you before it was instant arousal,' Christian murmured, against her mouth. 'And it is again.'

'The kissing was mutual,' she told him.

She felt him smile. 'And so is the arousal,' he said, his fingertips brushing across the tight points of her breasts and making her gasp.

As he continued to kiss her, his hands began to move in a voyage of discovery. He caressed her shoulders, the high curves of her breasts, the plane of her stomach, and finally his touch grazed across the soft furred mound between her thighs. Jocasta strained closer. An ache was growing, pulsing, and when he murmured, 'Which bed?' she smiled and whispered,

'Mine.'

Christian started to undress her. First her robe slithered rustling to the floor. Next he unhooked the shoestring straps from her shoulders, then he slid the nightgown from her body. And as the silk retreated he kissed and caressed the silken skin which was exposed.

When his hands rounded on her bared breasts, Jocasta arched hungrily towards him. He circled his thumbs across her nipples and, as she purred her pleasure, he bent his dark head and began to suckle her. At the caress of his tongue, riotous blood pounded in her head. Desire stung, and she moved restlessly against him. As Christian kicked away his briefs she put her hands on his hips, drawing him closer. The ache was begging for release.

'Wait,' he murmured.

'You're always telling me to wait,' Jocasta protested.

'But, honey, it's better this way,' he said, and slowly, slowly, his fingers began to stroke and caress again until in time her whole body seemed to be vibrating.

Yet although Christian's lovemaking was unhurried, there was a perpetual sense of tamed passion and a control reined tightly in which she found intensely exciting. It *was* better like this, Jocasta thought, and she began to kiss and explore and stroke him.

'Don't ever cut your hair,' he muttered, as she lowered her head and the long blonde strands drifted across his body. 'It's a wonderfully erotic accessory.'

Leisurely, she trailed her hand down his stomach and on to his thigh, and where her hand had been, her mouth followed. Christian submitted to the pleasure for a while, but then, with a groan, he moved her beneath him.

'I thought we were doing this slowly?' Jocasta smiled.

'Jo, everyone has their limits and I've reached mine,' he said, his eyes black with desire.

She felt the thrust of his male flesh inside her. Again, his hand came to her breast and as he touched her swollen nipples Jocasta cried out, lost in a sensual maelstrom. His thighs cleaved to hers in an urgent rhythm and her delighted whimpers were joined by his moans of satisfaction. A climax was coming, deeper and more profound than she had ever known before. Her fingernails biting into the smooth olive skin of his back, she clung to him.

'Now, Jo,' he said, in a low voice, *'now.'*

With a tremor which marked the peak of his need, Christian moved—making her head spin dizzily and sending her gasping and clutching and falling down, down, down into sublime satisfaction.

Jocasta opened her eyes and came slowly awake. For a while she lay there, bathed in happiness, then she raised her head to peer through the shadows at the clock on the bedside table. Its luminous fingers said five o'clock. There were another ten minutes before the alarm was due to ring—bliss! Smiling, she

snuggled deeper into the warm male body
which was wrapped around her.

After she and Christian had made love, they
had fallen asleep—and she had stayed asleep.
This was remarkable, she reflected, for no
matter how often she had slept with Oliver she
had never done so easily. Her subconscious, it
seemed, had regarded him as an intruder and
an alien, and invariably she had awoken in the
night. Then she had lain there, resenting the
sound of his breathing, irritated by his move-
ments, perversely wishing he would go and
leave her on her own. But for six hours she had
slept with Christian and slept at peace.

Carefully, she wriggled around to face him.
Although it was dark, the moon shone behind
the curtains and she could see his features in
the silvery light. With his lashes spread on his
cheeks and his hair tousled, he looked de-
fenceless and trusting. But that was what the
contented sharing of the sleep world meant, she
mused; a relinquishing of control and total ac-
ceptance. Jocasta rubbed her foot along his leg.
Sleeping with Christian felt as though it was
meant to be. Had they been lovers in an earlier
existence? she wondered.

As he murmured, she stretched out an arm
and switched on the bedside lamp. She wanted
to watch him awaken. She wanted to see that

first uninhibited moment of recognition. As Christian drowsily opened his eyes and looked at her, Jocasta felt a spurt of delight. He, too, she knew, had experienced that fleeting instinctive feeling of intimacy.

'Hello,' she said softly.

An emotion she could not define crossed his face.

'What time is it?' he asked.

'Just gone five.'

With a harsh expletive, Christian flung back the sheet and leapt from the bed. Finding his underpants, he hurriedly put them on.

'I must go,' he said.

Taken aback by this whirlwind of activity, Jocasta struggled up on to the pillow. 'But it only takes minutes to drive to the studios, so you've plenty of time for a shower and a cup of coffee.'

And to kiss me 'good morning', she added silently.

'I'm leaving now,' he declared, and strode away to the spare bedroom.

Pulling on her nightdress and robe, she padded out to the landing, only to find that Christian had already reappeared. He was fully dressed, though he looked rumpled and fidgety as though his clothes had been thrown on with the quickest possible speed.

'I realise this is your line,' Jocasta said, with a smile, 'but what's the hurry?'

'I need to go home and change before I start work,' he replied, the ends of his tie whipping through the air as he hastily tied the knot.

'I thought you kept a spare shirt in your office?'

A muscle clenched in his jaw. 'Quit the pressure.'

'I'm only suggesting you have a cup of coffee,' she protested.

'I don't want one!'

'Then don't have one,' Jocasta retorted, in a flare of tit for tat irritation. 'I know it's early and I'd never claim to be sweetness and light myself first thing, but, tell me, are you always this pleasant when you wake up?'

He glowered. 'The car'll be collecting you soon and what's the driver going to think if he finds me here?'

'Does it matter?'

'Yes, it damn well does!' Christian replied, in a voice which was almost a growl.

'So you go before he appears.'

'I'm leaving *now*.'

Jocasta looked at him. Where had all this anger come from? What made him so desperate to be gone? Why was his body language shouting out 'don't touch me'? A shiver went through her. She was, she realised, being exceedingly slow on the uptake.

'You might as well say it,' she told him, her tone abruptly icy.

His brow furrowed. 'Say what?'

'That I seduced you last night as I'm supposed to have seduced Mr Baumgarten.'

'I don't believe you did seduce him,' he said slowly.

'Huh!' The exclamation was sharp with disbelief. 'But you do think I slept with you because I hoped it might further my career with TKFM, and now you're regretting it like hell?'

'No. You've got it wrong. Well, I mean——' he frowned, struggling for words '—I am, though——'

Jocasta drew her robe closer around her throat. 'Don't worry, I regret last night, too,' she told him.

His eyes narrowed in surprise. 'You do?'

'Add sex to a working relationship and you add problems. Problems I don't want,' she declared, and the transparent relief which appeared on his face sliced into her like a razor. 'However, I wish to point out that the responsibility for last night lies with you,' she continued. 'It was *you* who suggested sleeping here and it was *you* who waylaid me when I was on my way to bed—alone! However, I am on the Pill, so you've no need to fear I'll become pregnant.'

Christian moistened his lips. 'Jo——'

'It was just one of those things, so let's leave it for now. Let's leave it for ever,' she said, and gestured towards the stairs. 'Shouldn't you be going?'

She might have been kissed and cruelly dismissed, but there would be no howls of outrage from her. No request that they talk things over. No running around like a headless chicken, hoping Christian might change his mind— about her seducing him or about him rejecting her. She had come to the States to learn, and, unfortunate though it was, what had happened would be marked down as a learning experience.

Christian hesitated for a moment. 'I guess so,' he muttered, and walked past her. 'See you later,' he said.

# CHAPTER SEVEN

I'VE missed my vocation, Jocasta thought wryly, later that morning— I should have been a meringue. On the outside she was sweet, inside she was hollow, and all it required was one unexpected knock and she would crumble into pieces. Yet, amazingly, her air-hostess smile and what she regarded as a robotic yo-ho-ho performance on *First Watch* had fooled everyone. Even Christian. On their meeting again he had been watchful, as though wondering whether second thoughts might have her slamming him against the wall and haranguing him. But, as time passed and she remained unflaggingly amiable, his tension had slackened. He might look a little haunted— Gaelene had speculated on his having had a late night—but he appeared to realise there would be no recriminations, and was grateful.

Courtesy of the 'compartment' method Jocasta had survived again, but as she let herself into the townhouse her shoulders sagged, her throat stiffened, her eyes grew misty. A deep breath was taken and her backbone straightened. She might have cried over Oliver, but she would not cry now. Before there had been the demise of a serious, year-long romance to grieve over and regret, but all she had shared with Christian McCoid was one lousy night! It had been a wonderful night, a little voice in her head annoyingly insisted, and she was forced to agree—but, even so, she refused to weep.

Instead, she summoned up a fantasy Christian and, as she had done before, embarked on a furious conversation. Although he'd said he did not believe she had made advances to Mr Baumgarten, he had lied. He also thought she had shared his bed for self-serving purposes. Why else would he have been so abrasive and uptight afterwards? However, both ideas were not only preposterous but deeply insulting. Did she look like, talk like, act like, the kind of woman who resorted to devious means to get what she wanted? No. Had he ever caught her attempting to entice or inveigle? Never. Did anyone else at TKFM harbour doubts about her integrity. Negative. They had the sense to recognise a true-blue member of society when they saw one—and so should he! For a person so smart in every other area, he was a dismal judge of character, Jocasta acidly informed him. And if he insisted on strangling a relationship which could have been so *good*, that was his misfortune!

For a day or two, these mental outbursts seemed to be essential to the functioning of her psyche and were endlessly and elaborately repeated, then she lost patience. Banging her head over someone with the perception of an idiot was a waste of time, Jocasta told herself, in a strict lecture. It must stop. And if she was bruised, she was far from bowed. After all, it was not as though she had fallen in love with Christian McCoid.

Nevertheless, he continued to bother her. She tried hard to become as inwardly negligent of him as her external manner suggested, but without success. All he needed to do was appear in the distance or utter an instruction through her earpiece, and her pulse jittered and her concentration was shot.

A few days later, when he asked her to remain at the end of a *First Watch* postmortem, Jocasta longed to refuse. A room full of people provided some kind of protection, but this would be the first time they had been alone since their lovemaking—and how did she cope? She swallowed hard. By being matter-of-fact and adult, of course. Christian was at his desk sorting through some papers, so she rose from the table and walked across to join him—on legs which had taken on the consistency of Plasticine.

'What do you want?' she enquired, a mite tartly, as the last person departed.

He pushed the papers aside. 'I was wondering whether you'd had any more phone calls.'

'Phone calls?'

'Nasty ones.'

'Oh . . . no.'

'How about being followed—has that happened again?'

'No.' Jocasta gave a careless laugh. 'Though I don't know that it happened the first time. Actually I now suspect it was all my imagination.' Like the affinity I thought we shared, she tacked on silently. 'I've been researching the Mardi Gras,' she continued, then stopped, frowning. 'I assume I am still on the team?'

'You think I'd change my mind?'

'You might,' she said coolly, remembering how he had changed it before—overnight.

Christian gave the ghost of a smile. 'I haven't.'

'I've been reading up on how the festival's reckoned to have its roots in the celebration of the Lupercalia, a pagan rite of spring which involved three days of mass orgies, and how the New Orleans carnival was started in the 1870s,' Jocasta said, chattering partly because she was nervous and partly because she needed to make it clear that her spare time had been spent working, not moping. 'I know there are fifty or more parades, and that when the crowds shout "Throw me something, mister", the people on the floats toss out handfuls of plastic beads or fake doubloons or small toys— and everyone tries to collect as many as they can. I'm swotting up on the different carnival clubs or "krewes", and——'

'The viewers sure won't be starved of information,' he cut in drily.

She flushed. 'No.'

'We need to work out who's doing what and where and when, so if everyone gathers here next——' Christian broke off as the door opened. 'Hi, Max,' he said, in surprise. 'I thought you were sailing the high seas?'

'Couldn't stand playing the stupid games and being buttonholed by blue-rinsed widows,' TKFM's owner grumbled, as he walked in, 'so I jumped ship at the first port of call.' He nodded at Jocasta. 'How ya doin'?'

'I'm fine, thank you,' she replied.

He indicated the box he was carrying. 'These are your video tapes,' he told her, and handed it over to Christian. 'I understand you're anxious to take a look,' he said, 'but I'd like them back when you've finished.'

Thanking him, Christian put the box on his desk and folded his arms. 'What's so special about these videos?' he enquired.

'Nothing.'

'Then why is it important they're returned?'

His employer fingered his droopy moustache. 'I want to watch them again,' he muttered.

'What for?'

He frowned. 'It's—um—interesting to compare the UK way of doing things with ours.'

'Come on, Max, you don't give a damn,' Christian protested, and shone a friendly man-to-man smile. 'You've not taken a shine to *First Watch*'s newest presenter, have you?'

Jocasta shot him a startled glance. She, too, would like to know the reason for Mr Baumgarten's interest in her tapes, but what line of questioning was this? Surely Christian didn't intend to claim the businessman was smitten and then work his way around to accusing her of sexual exploitation again? Her mouth thinned. Just let him try!

'A shine?' the visitor repeated, and his face gathered a pinky hue.

'It wouldn't be unusual,' Christian said easily. 'The studios have received hundreds of letters from guys of eighteen up to eighty, all claiming Jocasta as their number one pin-up, so—— '

'Not hundreds,' she cut in.

'Count them,' he instructed, and resumed his interrogation. 'Jocasta's your pin-up, too. Isn't she?'

Max Baumgarten dipped a finger into his collar and tugged, as though it had suddenly shrunk to a size too tight. 'It's not like that,' he mumbled.

'Don't misunderstand me, I'm not suggesting you're lusting after her,' Christian said, and frowned. 'All I'm asking is—is it her looks which appeal, and are they the reason for your watching the videos? And,' he added, 'are her looks the reason why you hired her?'

Suddenly recognising a chance to prove her innocence, Jocasta took a step forward. 'With regard to hiring me, it was your decision alone, wasn't it, Mr Baumgarten? I mean, I didn't...manipulate you in any way.'

'Manipulate?' he queried, looking puzzled.

'I didn't promote my own cause, or beg for a chance, or smile nicely, or——' Faced with her supposed victim, it had become a difficult word to say. She gulped in a breath. 'Seduce you?'

'Seduce me? For heaven's sake, no!' Max Baumgarten was shocked. 'Does someone think that?'

'Not now,' she said, and shot Christian a triumphant glance. 'But why did you hire me?' she enquired.

The pinky hue deepened.

'Own up,' Christian entreated.

Again, their employer tugged awkwardly at his moustache. 'I know you'll think this is dumb and overly sentimental—and not too complimentary,' he said, speaking to Jocasta, 'and I guess it is. But I hired you because you remind me of Rosie.'

'Rosie?' she asked.

'My daughter. You don't sound the same— so I play the videos with the sound turned down—but you look like her. Well, not exactly,' he amended, 'but near enough. Now-adays I only get to see her once or twice a year, so watching you is a substitute. Makes me feel closer to her. Happier.'

'The reason you offered Jocasta a job with TKFM is because she's a lookalike?' Christian protested.

Max Baumgarten gave a sheepish smile. 'Yes. I think she's a real skilled presenter,' he added hastily, 'but——'

Jocasta grinned. 'I don't mind.'

'And she is skilled,' Christian said. 'You made a good choice.'

'I did?' he asked, with unflattering surprise. 'Inspired.'

Able to relax now—and pleased with himself—TKFM's proprietor started to talk about the increased profits which his com-munications network looked like making that year. For a few minutes he quoted figures and percentages, then he departed.

'So, the mystery has been solved,' Christian said.

'Only because you kept on asking questions and refused to let Mr Baumgarten off the hook,' Jocasta remarked.

His brows came low. 'I needed to know,' he muttered.

She liked that. *Needing* to know meant that turning his back had been as painful for him as it had been for her, and now Christian would apologise and beg forgiveness. A warm feeling began to grow inside her. She would forgive him—how could she do otherwise?—but it would be slowly. She was not going to rush back into his arms. On the contrary, she would keep him waiting, hoping, fearing...and enjoy every deliciously agonising moment.

'Although Max rarely shows any interest in the programmes, he does keep a close eye on our finances,' Christian continued, sitting back behind his desk and gesturing for her to sit down, too. 'The guy knows exactly what's spent where and won't waste a dime, so to employ you when your deal included a generous salary, air fares *and* free accommodation made no sense at all.'

'Which was why you decided I must be guilty of foul play?'

'I couldn't work out how it had all come about,' he said, and sighed. 'So, yes, at first I did wonder whether you might have soft-soaped Max in some way. That's why I confined you to the sofa. OK, you were telegenic and had a pleasant manner, but, when it came to something serious, for all I knew you could have had more talent as a hustler than a television journalist.'

'It was only at first that you wondered whether I'd soft-soaped Mr Baumgarten?' Jocasta queried.

'That's right. I eventually realised I was way off beam. I did say I knew you hadn't,' he reminded her.

'Yes, but—but when was "eventually"?'

His mouth curved. 'You want the exact day? It was when you did your striptease, which must have been after you'd been here a month or so.'

'I did not do a striptease!'

Christian raised two hands. 'Sorry,' he said, grinning, 'but whatever you want to call it, that was when I knew I'd made a big mistake. Hell, you were so indignant when I suggested you might have seduced Max it was obvious you were telling the truth. And obvious you'd never seduce anyone.'

Jocasta stared at him. 'So you don't think that I——'

'Think you what?' he asked, when her words trailed away.

'Never mind,' she muttered, as her reasoning for his loving and leaving her went up in smoke.

'Next I told myself you were one of Max's eccentricities,' Christian carried on, 'but it never really jelled. So in the end I decided he must have hired you because he was enamoured.' He paused. 'To track back a bit, when I thought about his housekeeper saying how he watched your videos it struck me that Max might be having doubts about you—which is why I said not to feel too secure.'

'I thought *you* were the one with doubts,' Jocasta told him.

'No. By then, I knew you were a first-rate presenter and if Max had changed his mind——'

'As he changed it over the pond?'

'And with his cruise. If he had changed his mind I'd have argued against your dismissal, but he has the final word and could have enforced it.'

She considered this for a moment, then frowned. 'I wasn't aware you keep a check on my mail.'

'I don't,' Christian said, and turned his attention to the papers on the desk again. 'It was just that—well, I figured it might be interesting to read a few letters.'

'And was it?'

'No.' He hesitated. 'Not really.' He looked up. 'You didn't realise so many people write to you?'

Jocasta shook her head. 'You see, I've arranged for the secretaries to sift through and only pass on those letters which require a personal reply.'

'Why don't you read all your fan mail?' he asked.

'Two reasons. One, because I once worked with someone who did and whose ego rapidly became inflated.' She made a face. 'And two, because the explicit things some people put in their letters shocks me. I'm not a prude, but——'

'It can be strong stuff,' Christian agreed. 'When Max interrupted us I was talking about the Mardi Gras meeting. I'd like everyone to gather here at eleven a.m., Monday.'

'Fine,' she said, and rose. At the door, Jocasta halted. 'What was your wife like?' she enquired.

Christian had been bent over his papers again, but now his head jerked up as if she had tugged on a raw nerve.

'My wife?' he repeated, in a taut, muted voice.

With her 'seduction' theory debunked, she had been searching for another explanation for his behaviour the other morning, and now she had it. Martine had absorbed his thoughts at the time of his affair with Debra, and nothing had changed. Her stomach muscles tightened. She felt wretched. Now she understood his regrets and why he had walked out. Christian was still in love with his wife.

'Was she blonde, brunette or a redhead?' Jocasta asked, though the question was superfluous.

He realigned his blotter pad and several pens. 'She had dark hair. Cut short. With a fringe. Very chic. Very Parisian,' he said, speaking in terse, clipped phrases. 'She was pretty. Vivacious. Charmed everyone she met.'

It was glaringly obvious that he was not enjoying this, and neither was Jocasta. She did not want to hear how wonderful the French girl had been.

'I'll be at the Mardi Gras meeting,' she told him, and fled before he could say anything else.

Having come to the States to escape reminders of one broken relationship, Jocasta now found herself tortured by another. As the days passed, memories of Christian's lovemaking, his tenderness, the knowledge that they had been so *right* together, circled around and around in her head. After having told herself she did not love him, now she began to wonder. But what was the use of loving Christian when he remained in thrall to his dead wife?

Yet Jocasta knew she still attracted him. Whenever they met, the way his gaze lingered just a fraction too long, and the way so often when she looked at him she found he was looking at her, suggested she might be able to coax him back into bed. And, after that, into a relationship? It had no appeal. She would not tie herself to a man who yearned for another woman—and who might secretly yearn for her for the rest of his life. It was impossible to fight a ghost, and being a second-best love was not for her.

But seeing Christian every day became a form of punishment. Jocasta had never been neurotic, yet now she felt as brittle as glass. It was obvious this state of affairs could not continue, so what did she do? Tender her resignation as he had once suggested? But her career at TKFM was taking off and she liked working in America. Christian had talked about the Mardi Gras bringing her to the notice of other networks, and, although she felt this was a long shot, Jocasta decided to postpone any decision until after the carnival. Then, if she was offered another job in the States, she would take it. Otherwise—well, she might quit and head for home.

Fat Tuesday, and what had been billed as 'the greatest free show on earth', arrived. By now the city was bright with flags and ribbons in the carnival colours of green, gold and purple. By now, the streets were packed with jostling, merry people. By now, Jocasta had watched sufficient television coverage to know she was destined for twelve hours of fun, and very hard work.

Starting at noon—which made a pleasant change—she joined Chip and Ed on a camera platform towards the start of the parade route and, as the masked riders, the marching bands, the decorated floats with their papier-mâché sculptures went by, deftly began her commentary. Later, she dived into the crowds and buttonholed first a man in a tiger suit, then a jazz musician, then a visitor from Arkansas—and on and on. Around her people were yelling for throws, exchanging kisses for paper flowers, jitterbugging to the beat. Occasionally Christian's voice sounded in her ear, but today Jocasta had too much to do, too much to look at, too much to enjoy, to react.

The bawdy aspect of New Orleans' Mardi Gras surprised her. A plea for a float rider to 'throw something' was often rejoined with the flirtatious male instruction to 'show something' and several young women around her had obligingly displayed their breasts. When similarly entreated, Jocasta had laughingly refused. One accusation of performing a strip-tease was enough!

As darkness fell, she and the camera crew took time off for a quick meal, then made their way to the French Quarter. The area was a magnet for carnival-goers with the flashiest costumes, and zigzagging along the streets she saw feathered warriors, gold-laméd pirates, kings and queens in jewelled clothes. The scene here was wilder, the crowds thicker, and, as the evening progressed, interviews became a matter of Jocasta fighting her way into the crush—and fighting her way out again.

Sitting before the bank of screens in one of TKFM's control rooms, Gavin pointed a finger. 'See that beefy character munching a hamburger, the one off to the left? He was in the background on a couple of Jo's earlier interviews.'

'So he's following her around,' a production assistant dismissed. 'Some people are desperate to get their faces on television.'

'Yeah, just you wait and he'll start waving at the camera,' someone else put in scornfully.

Christian studied the man in question. 'Are you sure it's the same guy?' he asked Gavin.

'Wouldn't stake my life on it, but almost.'

The interview ended and transmission was switched to another reporter. It was another quarter of an hour before Jocasta reappeared on the monitor—this time talking to a different person in a different street.

'There you go, the guy's there again!' Gavin proclaimed. 'And this time I'm certain it's him.'

'Must be pretty determined to stick with her through those crowds,' remarked the assistant.

Christian examined the screen. Tucked in among the press of people behind her, the man was staring fixedly at Jocasta.

'Seems fascinated by her,' someone observed, in an echo of his thoughts.

'Got the hots,' Gavin chuckled, 'and who can blame him?'

Christian's brow furrowed. 'He looks familiar.'

'Not to me,' said his second in command.

'Anyone else recognise him?' he enquired hopefully, but all he received was a chorus of negatives. 'I'd swear I know him from somewhere.' He peered forward, racking his brain. 'Who is he?'

Time moved on. The man appeared in Jocasta's next broadcast, but when it came to eleven-thirty and her final slot he was nowhere in sight. Christian gave a sigh of relief. He had been wondering whether he ought to advise her of the man's presence, but had hesitated, wary of causing unnecessary alarm. After all, the man had only looked and in streets thronged with people she was not in any danger.

'The redneck's gone home to bed,' Gavin declared, yawning. 'And in another few minutes that's where I'm heading.'

As midnight approached one of the balls was featured, a camera went into a jazz club, and finally there were shots of the police cars which were preparing to cruise the French Quarter with the loudspeakered message that the Mardi Gras was over and everyone should leave. A few cutaways, 'goodbye's and 'thank you's, and TKFM's coverage came to an end.

Christian was walking with Gavin across the moonlit car park when suddenly he halted and uttered a savage expletive.

'The name of that guy,' he said. 'It's Roland Kleat.'

'Who's he?'

'Don't you remember, there was a lot about him in the papers a year or so back. He's a drifter and he'd been pursuing some young actress in Los Angeles, so she'd taken him to court. Apparently he had psychotic delusions about her being in love with him and had made threats when she didn't respond, and she was terrified he was going to assault her. She tried to have him locked up, but because he hadn't actually done anything a loophole in the law meant he could only be imprisoned for a certain number of days. The girl was so scared of him she quit the acting profession, changed her name and disappeared.'

'And she was from New Orleans,' Gavin said, now recalling the case. He looked at Christian in horror. 'Do you reckon Kleat came here looking for her and has fastened on to Jo instead?'

'Yes, I do.' He put a distraught hand to his head. 'And those letters I read—they were signed with an "R".'

'Which letters?' his companion asked, but Christian was already running towards his car.

'Phone Jocasta,' he shouted over his shoulder, 'and if she answers tell her to make sure her house is secured. I'll be there as quick as I can, but warn her not to open the door to anyone but me. If she's not there——' he vaulted into the car '—ring the police, explain she's in the French Quarter probably heading for home, and that a guy who's deranged could be tracking her. Do it now!' he barked.

Gavin blinked. 'Yes, sir.'

When their filming ended and Chip suggested she join him and Ed for a nightcap, Jocasta had happily agreed. It would be good to relax and talk the day through. Besides, the crowds had yet to disperse, and her journey home would be easier if she waited until the streets were less congested. But after one glass of wine the strain of the past hours caught up with her and she started to droop.

'Like me to see you to your door?' Chip asked, as she smothered a yawn.

Ed, who was younger and unmarried, put down his beer. 'Or me?' he grinned.

'No need,' she told them, reluctant to disturb what looked like becoming a dedicated drinking session. 'I only live a couple of blocks away.'

Pulling her coat over her sweater and miniskirt, Jocasta said goodbye. It was a quarter of an hour after midnight, but the hordes had scattered with surprising speed and already the streets were quiet. She doubted any of her interviews had been outstanding enough to garner interest from the other networks, Jocasta thought, as she walked along, but, even so, she would not have missed Mardi Gras for the world. It had been a memorable occasion. She grinned. And tomorrow Christian had excused her from *First Watch,* so she could have another lie-in. Entering the passageway, she unfastened her shoulder bag and fumbled around in its depths for her keys. Where were they? She had a reference book in her bag and everything was jammed inside. But perhaps she was underselling her interviews? The tiger-suited man had been articulate and witty, and, thanks to her research, she had been able to ask him a series of relevant questions. Maybe if one of the powers-that-be at——

A step into the silvered dark of the courtyard and octopus arms reached out from behind. Someone grabbed, jerking her violently backwards into what seemed like a large male body. The breath slammed from her lungs. Her bag went flying.

'Aarghh!' Jocasta gurgled, as greasy fingers impregnated with a hamburger smell clamped themselves across her mouth.

The bile rose in her throat. She almost gagged. For a moment, fright held her immobile then, struggling wildly, she started to fight for release. But all she achieved was a tightening of the fingers and the thick arm which bound her waist.

'You shouldn't have done it,' a voice hissed, beside her ear. 'Sending me all those messages, pretending you were mine, and then——' the hiss took on a jagged note '—cheating on me.'

Which messages? Jocasta wondered frantically. She had pretended she was his? What was he talking about?

'I won't have it, though you'll never do it again,' the voice went on. 'I shall save you from your errors, my angel. Tonight I shall achieve my sacred mission. And who can blame me?

Who can blame me for doing what needs to be done when it's the reason I was put on earth? I am here to save. I have been sent to save.'

As the man continued to chant in a maudlin, stream-of-consciousness kind of way, fear iced her blood and shivered her skin. He sounded unbalanced. 'Sacred mission'—what did he mean? How would he save her? Suddenly the arm around her waist was thrust behind her back and she felt a point jab between her shoulderblades. Her captor had a knife. Oh, God! He intended to kill her. Her stomach pitched and tossed. Her heart jabbered. Keep calm, she ordered herself, and think. Jocasta looked across to the townhouses. No lights shone, so any help must come from the street. But the street had been empty and, in any case, how did she get back there?

'My angel,' the man crooned again, and his grip eased. Not by much, but enough to allow a glimmer of hope.

Her overcoat was unfastened, so if she could divert his attention and slide out of it... Abruptly rearing back, Jocasta opened her mouth and bit into the greasy fingers. As the man swore, she wrenched herself from the coat and broke free. Run, her instincts screamed, run! Swerving past him, she dashed into the passage—and to her astonishment saw

Christian suddenly appear at the far end. She ran, he ran, and they met in the middle.

'Thank goodness you're here!' she gasped, collapsing into his arms.

'Are you all right?' he demanded, his tone agitated and his face ravaged.

She took a breath. 'I'm OK, but a man just grabbed me. He said I'd cheated on him and that—that I was his mission,' Jocasta told him, jabbering in her relief.

'This happened in the courtyard?' Christian enquired.

She looked back, but there was no sign of her captor. 'Yes.'

'Is there another exit?'

'No.'

'Go on to the street and wait,' he instructed.

Jocasta stared. 'While you give chase?' she protested, in horror.

'He was going to hurt you,' Christian said, in a low fierce voice, and made to go past her.

She clutched at his sleeve. 'Don't,' she pleaded. 'You mustn't. The man's dangerous. He has a knife.'

'The man's name is Roland Kleat,' Christian said, 'and if he isn't caught he's going to track you again. That's the way his mind works.'

'I don't care. You could get hurt.'

He removed her fingers from his arm. 'Wait in the street,' he insisted. 'The police should be here soon.'

'Then let them chase him,' she said, but Christian was already striding down the passage.

As he reached the courtyard he stopped and peered in, but obviously he saw nothing for, after a moment, he walked to the fountain where he stopped again and circled a cautious look around. Her heart in her mouth, Jocasta crept forward. Although the passage was the only exit, the wall which separated the town-houses from the older property could be scaled—if you were desperate. She hoped Roland Kleat had been desperate. She prayed he had gone.

But all of a sudden, a bellow of 'You! You!' sounded and a burly figure rushed out from beneath a darkly spreading tree. Jocasta gaped in alarm, then, as a blade glinted and the figure hurled itself at Christian, she sped into the courtyard. The two men were struggling. The knife gave Roland Kleat the advantage, but Christian was younger, fitter, quicker. A first downward slash was parried, and he managed to land a punch on his assailant's jaw. The bellow came again, and a renewed onslaught. The knife was raised, but, although Christian swerved sideways, this time it glanced against his shoulder. Ashen-faced, Jocasta watched on. Had he been slashed? It was too dark to see. For a third time, the blade shimmered and, holding it on high, his attacker advanced, forcing Christian back against the wall.

Jocasta's heart thumped. He was trapped. But she could not just stand there, she had to do *something*. Suddenly, she noticed her shoulderbag lying on the ground, the book still inside. Tiptoeing over, she picked it up and, by twisting the strap around her hand, fashioned a makeshift weapon. As Roland Kleat prepared to strike again, she rushed from behind and fiercely swung the bag at his head. He swayed, staggered off balance and fell. There was a loud crack as his head hit the paving stones.

'Did he stab you?' she demanded, her eyes flying anxiously to Christian.

He shook his head. 'Missed by a mile.'

Jocasta gave a sigh of relief, then turned to gaze down at the inert figure. 'It's the man who grinned at me across the street,' she said, and her eyes widened in dismay. 'I think I've killed him!'

Christian came and put his arms around her. 'I doubt it, though he's going to have one heck of a sore head when he wakes up,' he said, and, as if in confirmation, their attacker groaned.

'Coming in here after him was crazy,' Jocasta protested, feeling weak and shaky and very close to tears.

'Honey, I was so angry. All I knew was that I loved you, and no way would I allow the bastard to attack you and get away with it.'

She looked up at him. 'You—you love me?' she faltered.

'I do,' he said softly.

Jocasta smiled. 'And I love you, too,' she said, then turned as footsteps echoed in the passageway and two police officers suddenly appeared.

Christian grinned. 'You guys sure took your time,' he said.

# CHAPTER EIGHT

AFTER Roland Kleat had been unceremoniously hauled to his feet and handcuffed, Christian and Jocasta were asked if they would follow the squad car back to police headquarters. Charges needed to be placed and statements given. As they drove through the dark streets, Christian explained why he had realised she could be in danger, and when she heard how the drifter had been gaoled for pursuing another woman yet quickly released Jocasta was alarmed.

'Suppose he's back on the streets and hunting me down again in another month or so?' she protested.

'I thought you said you didn't care?' Christian reminded her wryly, and placed his hand on her knee. 'Jo, after being laid out cold, the guy's going to steer well clear of you in future,' he insisted, but she was not convinced.

It was only when the police chief told them that their attacker had been placed in a cell and was destined to remain behind bars for a long time to come that Jocasta felt able to relax.

'Kleat's possession of a lethal weapon and the two assaults mean that this time when he comes to trial he'll receive a hefty sentence,' the policeman assured her, 'so you can rest easy.'

She smiled. 'I'll try,' she said.

'And if any other nut takes it into his head to imitate Kleat he needn't bother,' Christian declared, 'because in future I intend to stick to you like glue.'

The police chief ran his eyes appreciatively over her, and winked. 'Sounds an enviable position to be in.'

'I should have warned you Kleat had been seen hanging around on your interviews,' Christian sighed, as they returned to the Porsche. Climbing in beside her, he took hold of her hand and started to play with her fingers as though they were worry beads. 'Everyone in the control room saw how absorbed in you he was and I knew I remembered him from somewhere, yet I did nothing—nothing!' he said, grimly berating himself.

'But you couldn't know he was planning to waylay me,' Jocasta protested.

'No, and yet I'd read enough of his letters to realise there was a crank on the loose. The dumb thing is, I'd checked your mail to discover just that.'

'Not to assess my popularity?' she asked.

Christian shook his head. 'I waded through it all because I'd decided maybe you *had* been followed, and also I was worried about that obscene phone call. But, having seen Kleat's letters, I then persuaded myself that even though ''R'' didn't have all his paddles in the water he was harmless!'

'But a proportion of the people who write in are cranks and ninety-nine per cent of the time there isn't any reason to worry,' Jocasta pointed out.

He sighed again. 'True.'

The police chief had relayed the gist of the drifter's statement to them, and she began to mull it over.

'Roland Kleat insists he didn't make the obscene call,' she said. 'I believe him. The voice was higher pitched.'

'Much,' Christian agreed. 'And, as he's owned up to the other two calls and how he'd been tracking you, I don't see any reason for him to lie about that. Some other guy ringing on the night he followed you home was just an unpleasant coincidence.'

'Kleat told the police he'd been tracking me virtually since I arrived, which must have been why he seemed familiar when I saw him at the dry cleaners,' Jocasta brooded. 'He was a face in the crowd which my subconscious had remembered—but I didn't.'

'Yet he grinned because he felt certain you were about to go across and thank him for the flowers. And when you ignored him, he took offence and departed.'

'He doesn't sound to have been overjoyed when he saw us kissing in the passageway, either. Which is why, when you went into the courtyard and he recognised you, he reacted so violently.'

'A quick-to-anger and jealous individual, our Mr Kleat,' Christian said pithily.

Jocasta cast him a look. 'It didn't occur to me until later, but when I received the flowers you thought they'd come from Mr Baumgarten?'

'I wondered. Max has never struck me as a Don Juan type, but——' His shoulders rose and fell. 'If only I'd told you about the letters,' he muttered, chastising himself again.

Jocasta reached forward and tapped a finger on the end of his nose. 'Stop it,' she rebuked. 'You're a hero. If you hadn't recognised Kleat and come to my rescue, I dread to think what would have happened.'

'I await a telegram of congratulation from the White House by the minute,' Christian said, in wry self-derision.

'I mean it,' she insisted, and curled a hand around his neck and kissed him. 'Thank you.'

He drew her closer. 'The rescuing was mutual. You really went to town with that bag, so thank *you*.' His lips found hers, and they were locked in an increasingly fervent embrace when he abruptly pulled away. 'We are under surveillance,' he warned.

A group of uniformed policemen who had been crossing the car park had halted and were peering in at them.

Jocasta grinned at Christian, then grinned at the officers—who all grinned back.

'I doubt they'll arrest us for . . . necking,' she said.

'No, but they could for——' He muttered something cruelly explicit in her ear.

She looked at him with large, innocent eyes. 'You reckon those few kisses might have developed into that?'

Christian rammed the car into gear. 'It was a distinct possibility,' he declared, and, with a squeal of tyres, he swung the Porsche out on to the road and headed for the French Quarter.

'It's creepy the way Roland Kleat believes I sent him secret signals,' Jocasta brooded, as they entered the townhouse. 'When I smiled at the camera the next morning he thought I was privately acknowledging receipt of the bouquet, and whenever I brushed my hair from my shoulder it was supposed to mean I knew he

was watching and was sending him my love.'
She shuddered. 'Yuck!'

Christian led her to the sofa and sat her
down. He took both her hands in his. 'Jo, it's
over,' he said.

'Yes.'

'I realise you've been feeling uneasy for
weeks and being grabbed tonight must've given
you one hell of a fright, but——'

'Watching Kleat come at you with the knife
was worse,' Jocasta protested.

'OK, but now you're safe. We're both safe.'

'Yes,' she said, and this time the word was
firm.

Christian smiled. 'That's my girl. And don't
worry, because you're not going to walk
through that passageway in the dark on your
own ever again. I shall be with you. I'll move
my clothes round here tomorrow, then when
my house is ready we'll switch to there.'

'We will?'

'Don't get me wrong,' he said, 'I'm not
asking you to live in sin—yes, I am, though
not for long. What I'm really asking is, will
you marry me?'

Joy burst inside her like a shower of fire-
works, but a moment later Jocasta ordered
herself to come down to earth. Did she want
to be a second-string Mrs McCoid? Was she
willing to fill the place of Christian's French

wife—or attempt to fill it? She had believed the answer to be a decisive no, and yet now... When he said he loved her, she believed him. The problem was, how *much*? As deeply as he had loved, and still loved, Martine? Whether or not, wasn't being the runner-up in his affections by far preferable to coming first with someone who must necessarily be *her* second choice? She frowned. Such questions were a waste of time. The desire to spend the rest of her life with him allowed no choice.

Jocasta opened her mouth, but before she could speak he pulled back.

'What's the matter?' he demanded.

'Nothing.'

'There is.' Christian moistened his lips. 'I thought you said you loved me?'

'I do.'

'Then what's the hang-up about our getting married?'

Jocasta gave a silent scream. When she performed on air he was alert to every nuance, every fault, and now he had sensed her hesitation. Why must he be so astute?

'There isn't one.' Her smile dazzled. 'And the answer is yes, I'll marry you.'

'Like hell you will!' Christian rasped. 'Not if you have doubts.'

Her stomach churned. What did she say? Should she keep her worries concealed in a balloon over her head and hope to lie her way through? Or was it preferable to be honest and open? She dithered. Right now, either way seemed like a no-win situation.

Ostentatiously, Jocasta inspected her watch. 'It's one-thirty, so maybe we should talk about this tomorrow?' she suggested. 'I don't have to be up early in the morning, but you——'

'Don't either,' Christian cut in. 'When you were busy with the cops I rang the studios and left a message to say I wouldn't be in until late.'

'Then—um—suppose we have a brandy?' she suggested, playing for time in the hope that inspiration might arrive and tell her how to respond. 'I bought some,' Jocasta said, when he looked surprised. She gave a weak smile. 'Thought I'd better—for use in emergencies.'

This was an emergency, she thought, as she splashed the liquid into crystal goblets. A *dire* one. She handed Christian his drink and sat down again beside him. Taking a sustaining sip, she decided that, as the chances of his believing her if she lied were minimal, she had no option but to tell the truth. And if in being truthful she happened to discover that she came a *very* poor second to his first wife, it was something she would need to learn to live with.

'I realise that—that when someone you love dies your love doesn't die with them, and I would never expect it to,' she began hesitantly.

Christian frowned. 'Is that a reference to Martine and me?' he enquired.

'Yes.'

'Martine's the reason why you hesitated?'

'Yes,' she said again.

'Jo, I don't love her. In fact, it's not all that long since I stopped hating her.'

Mystified, Jocasta looked at him. 'But—but surely you told Debra you weren't interested in a serious relationship because you were still emotionally wound up in your wife?'

'Actually I didn't; she assumed it. Though it's immaterial, because I *was* wound up in her, but because of my hatred.'

'You hated Martine?' she protested, finding the assertion difficult to absorb.

'Violently, hands-on, from the day she died and roughly for the next eighteen months or so; which was a darn sight more than she ever deserved and far more than was good for me. It was a symptom of what's called post traumatic stress disorder.' Christian took a swift slug of brandy. 'Debra didn't know how I felt, neither did my folks nor any of my friends, come to that—and they still don't. Nobody knows, because I haven't told anyone. Until now.'

'Why did it start on the day she died?' Jocasta asked curiously.

'Because Martine was killed in her lover's car, when he was driving her back from an hotel where they'd shared an afternoon of illicit passion.'

'And you had no idea?'

'That she was cheating on me and had been for the past year?' he said, with a twisted smile. 'None.'

Jocasta put out a hand and touched his arm. Coping with any bereavement was difficult enough, but to be simultaneously confronted with his wife's adultery would have doubled the tragedy. She could well imagine how shocked he must have been, how confused, how hurt.

'Was the—the man killed, too?' she asked.

'No. His only injury was a broken arm. The other day you asked what Martine was like. She was everything I said, plus she was spoiled, selfish, and an eternal child.' Christian sighed. 'I'd better tell it from day one.'

'Please.'

He had another drink. 'I first met her when I was attending college in Paris. Her mother was a friend of my mother's, and when she heard I'd be studying over there she insisted I get in touch. Martine was around fifteen at the time.'

'How old were you?' Jocasta enquired.

'Twenty. Enough of the older man for her to develop a crush on me,' he said drily.

'And you fell in love with her?'

'Not then. As far as I was concerned, she was just a kid. A pretty one, yet a kid nevertheless. But her folks were friendly and hospitable and kept on inviting me round, and every time I visited their home she was there; the only child who'd been born late in their marriage and was adored and indulged.' Christian sipped again at his brandy. 'However, eight years or so later her parents unfortunately died within a few months of each other, and because Martine was going through a rough time my mother wrote and invited her over to New Orleans for a holiday. On her arrival, she rapidly made it plain that the crush remained and, with what seemed like amusing frankness, came after me. And now, in addition to being pretty, she was graceful, stylish, sexy.'

'You were flattered?' she asked.

'Naturally, and I started thinking about Martine in terms of love and marriage.' He frowned down into his glass. 'I've tried to analyse why, and I figure there were a number of reasons. None of which would have been sufficient on their own, but put together——' He sighed. 'If someone demonstrates they like you, then there's a tendency to like them back. And Martine's feeling so lost without her parents brought out my protective instincts. Also I was in my late twenties and several of my friends had recently got hitched, so it seemed like the time to settle down. Plus it didn't help any that my mother, who had always hoped my brother and I would marry French girls, had launched into a matchmaking routine. Martine's three-week vacation stretched to two months and——'

'Didn't she need to return to work?' Jocasta interrupted.

'No. At that point she was manageress of a dress shop, but the job wasn't important to her and when my mother suggested she extend her stay she phoned one morning and merrily informed them she wasn't coming back. Which should have alerted me to the fact that we were two very different people,' Christian said flatly, 'because, like you, I've always cared about my work. However, pretty soon we were married.'

'At which point you moved to France?'

He shook his head. 'I had an interesting job which offered excellent advancement with one of the New Orleans networks, and before the wedding we'd talked things over and agreed that our future was here. Martine had declared herself happy at the prospect of living in the States, but we were barely back from honeymoon before she started to complain of being homesick. She insisted she must see her friends again, so she went off to France for several weeks, came back and continued to be homesick. She hadn't got around to finding herself a job and, when I suggested it would help her settle down if she did, she sulked and said there weren't any jobs worth having. She also said New Orleans was a dismal town——'

'Dismal!' Jocasta protested.

'—and that our apartment was too small. Day after day I'd return home from work and find her sobbing.' Christian swirled the golden liquid in his glass. 'The upshot was that I quit my job and we switched to Paris.'

'I realise your French is fluent, but wasn't it difficult to fit into a different language television scene?' she asked.

He nodded. 'For a long time I was like a fish out of water.'

'But Martine was happy?'

'Martine was always happy when she'd got what she wanted,' he said sardonically. 'Her parents had left her a chunk of cash, and she insisted we buy an apartment in a swank *arrondissement*. I wasn't in agreement because, one, the place was far bigger and grander than we needed, and, two, rightly or wrongly, I believed it was up to me to support us and my resources didn't stretch anywhere near that far. However, Martine sulked and sobbed again, and I gave way.' He expelled a breath.

'I was beginning to realise just how spoiled she was.'

'If her parents had indulged her, it would have been a hard habit to break,' Jocasta observed.

'I know,' he said ruefully. 'Maybe if she'd been more mature she would've been willing to learn the art of compromise, but, as I said, Martine was the perpetual child. She may have looked chic and sophisticated, but inside she was still fifteen years old. When we moved into the apartment she was ecstatic, but she soon started to complain about the work involved in looking after it—even though we had a maid. A maid whom she'd insisted *I* must hire, because she didn't know how to go about it. But,' he said wearily, 'there were a hundred and one things she reckoned she couldn't do and which I had to do for her—as her father had done them before me.'

She eyed him quizzically. 'Do you think that could have been partly why Martine'd fallen in love with you? Because she felt adrift when her parents had died and you're a strong, capable kind of person?'

'I'm sure it was the *major* part. But, as for love, frankly I don't know whether her crush on me ever went beyond a crush. In fact, I doubt she was capable of love, not the true,

pulling-together kind.' Christian looked down
at his empty glass. 'This talking is thirsty work.'

'Would you like another brandy?'

He grinned. 'Please.'

Jocasta replenished his drink, but poured
herself some mineral water.

'So you reckon Martine had been looking for
a replacement father?' she prompted, as she sat
down again.

'Yes, but my view of marriage is a part-
nership, in which each person contributes
equally as an adult. I didn't want someone who
expected to be pampered and constantly spoon-
fed,' Christian said, and grinned. 'I wanted a
wife who, when faced with a problem, didn't
give up until she was certain there was no way
around it.'

Smiling, Jocasta laid her head on his
shoulder. 'Me.'

'The hell-on-wheels girl herself,' he said, and
kissed her. 'Back in Paris Martine found herself
a job in a shop, but soon quit and moved on
to another, complaining of being bored,' he
went on. 'She'd left school young on a whim
and lacked qualifications, so I, in my wisdom,
said why didn't she enrol at college and acquire
some and thus widen her career choice?' He
raised his eyes. 'Did that go down like a lead
balloon!'

'So the succession of jobs continued?'

'And the boredom. At one stage she became very keen on our having a child, but it was obvious she was simply seeking an alternative to work and I refused.'

'Martine sobbed and sulked again?' Jocasta enquired.

'Only briefly, because at heart she knew as well as I did that she wouldn't have enjoyed the demands a child would have made and would have resented it.'

'Was boredom the reason why she took a lover?'

Christian shook his head. 'I figure the need was more basic. You see, although I didn't enjoy playing "daddy", for two or three years I went along with it. I wanted to keep her happy, and Martine could be incredibly charming when she tried,' he explained. 'But in time I rebelled and refused to co-operate. This didn't cause any serious rows—her forte was sulking—but it did create a gap between us.' He frowned. 'I've thought about her infidelity a lot, and I reckon that when it dawned on her that I wasn't the father figure she needed and never would be she started to look elsewhere. Maybe not consciously, but when she met Robert, who was balding, plump, assertive and fifty-five, he must have seemed tailor-made and impossible to resist,' he remarked drily.

Jocasta sipped from her glass. 'Now I understand why you thought I might have seduced Mr Baumgarten.'

'Martine's seducing a guy like Robert made it seem possible,' he agreed. 'And, according to him, she did seduce him. I arrived at the hospital soon after the crash and, maybe because he was in shock, he not only immediately confessed to their affair but insisted on filling me in on all the details.'

She winced. 'That must have been hard to take.'

'As if I was being disembowelled. Robert said Martine had gone all out for him, the way she'd gone all out for me. OK, he was married—his wife owned one of the shops Martine had worked in—but she was young and beautiful, so—' He shrugged.

'Didn't he wonder why she should be attracted to him?'

'He knew. Apparently she'd talked about her father and how much she missed him, and Robert had realised he'd taken his place, though it didn't bother him. What he was concerned about was his wife discovering he'd been unfaithful. He asked if we could please tell everyone he'd innocently seen Martine in the street and offered her a lift, and as I saw no reason to upset the woman I agreed. Though the deception suited me, too,' he added.

'Everyone believed Martine and I had a good marriage, and I didn't relish the pity I'd have received if it had become known she'd been fooling around.'

Jocasta drank from her glass. 'You'd never been tempted to do the same?'

'No. I kept soldiering on, hoping Martine would grow up, hoping things would improve. And if I'd been asked at any time during our marriage whether it was happy I'd have said yes because, like everyone else, I'm not comfortable with the feeling of failure. I never seriously admitted to myself how rocky things were, and yet I suspect another reason why I didn't want a child was because, at the back of my mind, I had doubts about whether the marriage would last.'

'You said that after the accident, you hated France. Was that because of your feelings about Martine?'

Christian nodded. 'I'd enjoyed living there and once I'd got to grips I'd also enjoyed my job. However, the circumstances of her death smashed the illusions I'd had about our marriage and made me feel as though I'd lost all control. I couldn't trust anyone any more. Coming back to New Orleans was the equivalent of wrapping myself up in a blanket, I guess, though I found myself constantly reliving the past, dreaming about Martine, having sudden flashbacks to my conversation with Robert.'

'His being fat and bald couldn't have helped,' Jocasta reflected.

'It didn't. For a long while I couldn't understand why she'd chosen a middle-aged guy like him in preference to a young guy like me, and so part of my distress was due to my ego leading me around by the nostrils. I don't claim to be God's gift, but——'

'You are *gorgeous,*' Jocasta assured him.

He kissed her again. 'Not as gorgeous as you. But, to finish, although I eventually came to terms with Martine's adultery and understood why it had happened, the scar tissue remained and I vowed never to let a woman into my life again—not in any serious way. Which is why I was so wrought-up the morning after we'd made love,' Christian told her ruefully. 'Not only had I broken a golden rule about not staying the night, but in that first second of awakening I felt . . . a little bit married to you.'

'Hence the panic?'

He grinned. 'It was a mega terror attack.'

'One which lasted until today?'

'One which caused me a great deal of anguish because, if I was honest with myself, I knew we had something special going for us, but which lasted until I realised Kleat might be tracking you and you could get hurt.' He groaned. 'Did that clear my mind beautifully! In a split second, I knew I loved you and I needed you. I knew I had to go to bed with you each night and wake up with you every morning for the rest of my life. And I knew that if I lost you I'd die.' Christian took hold of her hand. 'Will you marry me?'

Jocasta did not hesitate this time. 'Yes, please.'

He put down their glasses and drew her close. Much kissing and holding and touching followed. Clothes were discarded, the temperature grew fevered, desire began to spiral.

'Bed,' Christian decreed, and wryly eyed the garments scattered on the floor. 'We've more or less undressed each other, so we are ready.'

'I thought that brandy was followed by a scrub-down in a hot bath?' she grinned.

'Honey, I want to make love to you, now. I *need* to,' he insisted.

Her eyes sparkled. 'Slowly?'

'It'll be slower the time after,' Christian said, and drew her with him up the stairs.

Rose crystals were swirled into the flow of warm water. Christian sat at the tapless end of the bath, with Jocasta in front of him. As his arms came around her, she nestled back.

'Those were the most exciting fifteen seconds of my life,' she grinned.

He took a mock bite at her shoulder. 'Twenty, but you don't expect me to be a model of restraint every time? Hell, Jo, you arouse me like crazy,' he protested.

'Ditto,' she smiled.

'You realise there are going to be loud shouts of favouritism when word about our relationship gets out and when I switch you to the evening news programme?' he enquired.

Jocasta twisted round to give a wide smile. 'Oh, Chris, thank you,' she said, and kissed him.

For a few minutes they lay together drowsily, enjoying the silky warmth of the water and the fragrant steam, then Christian found the soap. As he began to lather her, Jocasta sighed, submitting to the languorous pleasure as his hands slithered over her.

'When I asked you if I could interview the writer, do you think maybe I was pushing?' she enquired. 'Just a bit?'

'No way, it was a legitimate request,' he said, and continued to soap her, his hands sliding sensually over her breasts, her stomach, her thighs. 'You know who I'm beginning to remind myself of?' Christian said, after a while.

'Who?'

'Al the alligator, languishing for lack of love.'

She twisted to smile at him. 'You want us to go back to bed again *already*?'

'Don't you?'

Jocasta's reply was to reach forward and let out the water.

'If we call your folks in the morning, maybe they could find out what's involved in the legalities of us getting married,' Christian said, as they dried themselves. 'And the soonest a ceremony can take place.' He dispensed with his towel and drew her close, his hand resting below the curve of her breast where her heart beat. 'How do you fancy an Easter wedding?'

'But that's only six weeks away,' she said.

'Would you like to be married at Easter?' he insisted.

She laughed. 'Yes.'

'And how about kids? We'll leave it for a couple of years, but suppose we have four?'

'Four?' she protested.

'Or five. Or six. Or seven.' The Michelangelo lips curved. 'It's a legitimate request.'

Jocasta wrapped her arms around his neck. 'On the contrary, my beloved Christian,' she said, 'that is what is called pushy!'

# JAYNE ANN KRENTZ

A two-part epic tale from one of today's most popular romance novelists!

---

## Dreams
### Parts One & Two

*The warrior died at her feet, his blood running out of the cave entrance and mingling with the waterfall. With his last breath he cursed the woman— told her that her spirit would remain chained in the cave forever until a child was created and born there....*

So goes the ancient legend of the Chained Lady and the curse that bound her throughout the ages—until destiny brought Diana Prentice and Colby Savager together under the influence of forces beyond their understanding. Suddenly they were both haunted by dreams that linked past and present, while their waking hours were filled with danger. Only when Colby, Diana's modern-day warrior, learned to love, could those dark forces be vanquished. Only then could Diana set the Chained Lady free....

---

**Available in September wherever Harlequin books are sold.**

JK92

# HARLEQUIN
# *Romance*

**HARLEQUIN ROMANCE
IS BETTING ON LOVE!**

And The Bridal Collection's
September title is a sure bet.

**JACK OF HEARTS (#3218)
by Heather Allison**

# THE BRIDAL COLLECTION

**THE BRIDE** played her part.
**THE GROOM** played for keeps.
**THEIR WEDDING** was in the cards!

Available in August in
THE BRIDAL COLLECTION:

**THE BEST-MADE PLANS (#3214)
by Leigh Michaels**

Harlequin Romance

Wherever Harlequin
books are sold.

# WELCOME TO

**The quintessential small town, where everyone knows everybody else!**

Finally, books that capture the pleasure of tuning in to your favorite TV show!

**GREAT READING...GREAT SAVINGS...AND A FABULOUS FREE GIFT!**

Each book set in Tyler is a self-contained love story; together, the twelve novels stitch the fabric of the community. The covers honor the old American tradition of quilting; each cover depicts a patch of the large Tyler quilt.

With Tyler you can receive a fabulous gift, ABSOLUTELY FREE, by collecting proofs-of-purchase found in each Tyler book. And use our special Tyler coupons to save on your next TYLER book purchase.

Join your friends at Tyler for the seventh book, ARROWPOINT by Suzanne Ellison, available in September.

*Rumors fly about the death at the old lodge! What happens when Renata Meyer finds an ancient Indian sitting cross-legged on her lawn?*

---

If you missed *Whirlwind* (March), *Bright Hopes* (April), *Wisconsin Wedding* (May), *Monkey Wrench* (June), *Blazing Star* (July) or *Sunshine* (August) and would like to order them, send your name, address, zip or postal code, along with a check or money order for $3.99 for each book ordered (please do not send cash), plus 75¢ postage and handling ($1.00 in Canada), payable to Harlequin Reader Service, to:

| In the U.S. | In Canada |
|---|---|
| 3010 Walden Avenue | P.O. Box 609 |
| P.O. Box 1325 | Fort Erie, Ontario |
| Buffalo, NY 14269-1325 | L2A 5X3 |

Please specify book title(s) with your order.
Canadian residents add applicable federal and provincial taxes.

TYLER-7